"You still haven't answered my question—about marrying me," Troy said quietly.

Angelica glanced away.

"Have you thought about it?"

She shut her eyes for a moment. "I've hardly thought of anything else."

"And?"

"And…I don't know."

"Fair enough," he said. "But is there anything I could do to help you decide?"

She gave him a narrow-eyed look, and for a moment, he thought she was going to scold him. "Yes," she said finally. "You could tell me why you want to do it."

Should he tell her how much he'd started caring for her, or would that make her shy away?

Knowing her, it would. "That's easy. I want to do it because your son wants a dad. And because I like helping you."

Her mouth got a pinched look. If he hadn't known better, he'd have thought she felt hurt. "Those aren't…those aren't the reasons people get married."

"Are they bad reasons, though?"

She shook her head, staring at the ground. "They're not bad, no. They're fine. Kind. Good."

"Then what's standing in the way?"

She shrugged, looked away.

But he saw that there was a fine film of tears over her eyes.

Lee Tobin McClain read *Gone with the Wind* in the third grade and has been a hopeless romantic ever since. When she's not writing angst-filled love stories with happy endings, she's getting inspiration from her church singles group, her gymnastics-obsessed teenage daughter and her rescue dog and cat. In her day job, Lee gets to encourage aspiring romance writers in Seton Hill University's low-residency MFA program. Visit her at leetobinmcclain.com.

Books by Lee Tobin McClain

Love Inspired

Engaged to the Single Mom

Engaged to the Single Mom

Lee Tobin McClain

Recycling programs
for this product may
not exist in your area.

LOVE INSPIRED BOOKS

ISBN-13: 978-0-373-87948-9

Engaged to the Single Mom

And we know that all things work together for good to them that love God, to them who are the called according to His purpose.
—*Romans 8:28*

I owe much appreciation to my Wednesday-morning critique group—Sally Alexander, Jonathan Auxier, Kathy Ayres, Colleen McKenna and Jackie Robb—for being patient through genre shifts while gently insisting on excellence. Thanks also to my colleagues at Seton Hill University, especially Michael Arnzen, Nicole Peeler and Albert Wendland, whose support and encouragement keep me happily writing. Ben Wernsman helped me brainstorm story ideas, and Carrie Turansky read an early draft of the proposal and critiqued it most helpfully. I'm grateful to be working with my agent, Karen Solem, and my editor, Shana Asaro—dog lovers both—who saw the potential of the story and helped me make it better. Most of all, thanks belong to my daughter, Grace, for being patient with her creative mom's absentmindedness and for offering inspiration, recreation and eye-rolling, teenage-style love every step of the way.

Chapter One

"You can let me off here." Angelica Camden practically shouted the words over the roar of her grandfather's mufflerless truck. The hot July air, blowing in through the pickup's open windows, did nothing to dispel the sweat that dampened her neck and face.

She rubbed her hands down the legs of the full-length jeans she preferred to wear despite the heat, took a deep breath and blew it out yoga-style between pursed lips. She could do this. Had to do it.

Gramps raised bushy white eyebrows as he braked at the top of a long driveway. "I'm taking you right up to that arrogant something-or-other's door. You're a lady and should be treated as one."

No chance of that. Angelica's stomach churned at the thought of the man she was about to face. She'd fight lions for her kid, had done the equivalent plenty of times, but this particular lion terrified her, brought back feelings of longing and shame and sadness that made her feel about two inches tall.

This particular lion had every right to eat her alive. Her heart fluttered hard against her ribs, and when she took a deep breath, trying to calm herself, the truck's exhaust fumes made her feel light-headed.

I can't do this, Lord.

Immediately the verse from this morning's devotional, read hastily while she'd stirred oatmeal on Gramps's old gas stove, swam before her eyes: *I can do all things through Him who gives me strength.*

She believed it. She'd recited it to herself many times in the past couple of difficult years. She could do all things through Christ.

But this, Lord? Are you sure?

She knew Gramps would gladly go on the warpath for her, but using an eighty-year-old man to fight her battles wasn't an option. The problem was hers. She'd brought it on herself, mostly, and she was the one who had to solve it. "I'd rather do it my own way, Gramps. Please."

Ignoring her—of course—he started to turn into the driveway.

She yanked the handle, shoved the truck door open and put a booted foot on the running board, ready to jump.

"Hey, careful!" Gramps screeched to a stop just in front of a wooden sign: A Dog's Last Chance: No-Cage Canine Rescue. Troy Hinton, DVM, Proprietor. "DVM, eh? Well, he's still a—"

"Shhh." She swung back around to face him, hands braced on the door guards, and nodded sideways toward the focus of her entire life.

Gramps grunted and, thankfully, lapsed into silence.

"Mama, can I go in with you?" Xavier shot her a pleading look—one he'd perfected and used at will, the rascal—from the truck's backseat. "I want to see the dogs."

If she played this right, he'd be able to do more than just see the dogs during a short visit. He'd fulfill a dream, and right now Angelica's life pretty much revolved around helping Xavier fulfill his dreams.

"It's a job interview, honey. You go for a little drive with Gramps." At his disappointed expression, she reached back to pat his too-skinny leg. "Maybe you can see the dogs later, if I get the job."

"You'll get it, Mama."

His brilliant smile and total confidence warmed her heart at the same time that tension attacked her stomach. She shot a glance at Gramps and clung harder to the truck, which suddenly felt like security in a storm.

He must have read her expression, because his gnarled hands gripped the steering wheel hard. "You don't have to do this. We can try to get by for another couple of weeks at the Towers."

Seeing the concern in his eyes took Angelica out of herself and her fears. Gramps wasn't as healthy as he used to be, and he didn't need any extra stress on account of her. Two weeks at the Senior Towers was the maximum visit from relatives with kids, and even though she'd tried to keep Xavier quiet and neat, he'd bumped into a resident who used a walker, spilled red punch in the hallway and generally made too much noise. In other words, he was a kid. And the Senior Towers was no place to raise a kid.

They'd already outstayed their welcome, and she knew Gramps was concerned about it. She leaned back in to rub his shoulder. "I know what I'm doing. I'll be fine."

"You're sure?"

She nodded. "Don't worry about me."

But once the truck pulled away, bearing with it the

only two males in North America she trusted, Angelica's strength failed her. She put a hand on one of the wooden fence posts and closed her eyes, shooting up a desperate prayer for courage.

As the truck sounds faded, the Ohio farmland came to life around her. A tiny creek rippled its way along the driveway. Two fence posts down, a red-winged blackbird landed, trilling the *oka-oka-LEE* she hadn't heard in years. She inhaled the pungent scent of new-mown hay.

This was where she'd come from. Surely the Lord had a reason for bringing her home.

Taking another deep breath, she straightened her spine. She was of farm stock. She could do this. She reached into her pocket, clutched the key chain holding a cross and a photo of her son in better days, and headed toward the faint sound of barking dogs. Toward the home of the man who had every reason to hate her.

As the sound of the pickup faded, Troy Hinton used his arms to lift himself halfway out of the porch rocker. In front of him, his cast-clad leg rested on a wicker table, stiff and useless.

"A real man plays ball, even if he's hurt. Get back up and into the game, son." His dad's words echoed in his head, even though his logical side knew he couldn't risk worsening his compound fracture just so he could stride down the porch steps and impress the raven-haired beauty slowly approaching his home.

Not that he had any chance of impressing Angelica Camden. Nor any interest in doing so. She was one mistake he wouldn't make again.

His dog, Bull, scrabbled against the floorboards beside him, trying to stand despite his arthritic hips. Troy sank back down and put a hand on the dog's back. "It's okay, boy. Relax."

He watched Angelica's slow, reluctant walk toward his house. Why she'd applied to be his assistant, he didn't know. And why he'd agreed to talk to her was an even bigger puzzle.

She'd avoided him for the past seven years, ever since she'd jilted him with a handwritten letter and disappeared not only from his life, but from the state. A surge of the old bitterness rose in him, and he clenched his fists. Humiliation. Embarrassment. And worse, a broken heart and shattered faith that had never fully recovered.

She'd arrived in her grandfather's truck, but the old man had no use for him or any of his family, so why had he brought her out here for her interview? And why wasn't he standing guard with a shotgun? In fact, given the old man's reputation for thrift, he'd probably use the very same shotgun with which he'd ordered Troy off his hardscrabble farm seven years ago.

Troy had come looking for explanations about why Angelica had left town. Where she was. What her letter had meant. How she was surviving; whether she was okay.

The old man had raved at him, gone back into the past feud between their families over the miserable acre of land he called a farm. That acre had rapidly gone to seed, as had Angelica's grandfather, and a short while later he'd moved into the Senior Towers.

In a way, the old man had been abandoned, too, by the granddaughter he'd helped to raise. Fair warning. No matter how sweet she seemed, no matter what promises she made, she was a runner. Disloyal. Not to be counted on.

As Angelica approached, Troy studied her. She was

way thinner than the curvy little thing she'd been at twenty-one. Her black hair, once shiny and flowing down her back in waves, was now captured in a careless bun. She wore baggy jeans and a loose, dusty-red T-shirt.

But with her full lips and almond-shaped eyes and coppery bronze skin, she still glowed like an exotic flower in the middle of a plain midwestern cornfield. And doggone it if his heart didn't leap out of his chest to see her.

"Down, boy," Troy ordered Bull—or maybe himself—as he pushed up into a standing position and hopped over to get his crutches.

His movements must have caught the attention of Lou Ann Miller, and now she hobbled out the front screen door.

She pointed a spatula at him. "You get back in that chair."

"You get back in that kitchen." He narrowed his eyes at the woman who'd practically raised him. "This is something I have to do alone. And standing up."

"If you fall down those steps, you'll have to hire yet another helper, and you've barely got the charm to keep me." She put her hands on bony hips. "I expect you to treat that girl decent. What I hear, she's been through a lot."

Curiosity tugged at him. People in town were too kind to tell him the latest gossip about Angelica. They danced around the subject, sparing his ego and his feelings.

What had Angelica been through? How had it affected her?

The idea that she'd suffered or been hurt plucked at the chords of his heart, remnants of a time he'd have moved mountains to protect her and care for her. She'd had such a hard time growing up, and it had made him feel ten feet tall that she'd chosen him to help her escape her rough past.

Women weren't the only ones who liked stories of knights in shining armor. Lots of men wanted to be heroes as well, and Angelica was the kind of woman who could bring out the heroic side of a guy.

At least for a while. He swallowed down his questions and the bad taste in his mouth and forced a lightness he didn't feel into his tone. "Who says I won't treat her well? She's the only person who's applied for the job. I'd better." Looking at his cast, he could only shake his head. What an idiot he'd been to try to fix the barn roof by himself, all because he didn't want to ask anyone for help.

"I'll leave you alone, but I'll know if you raise your voice," Lou Ann warned, pointing the spatula at him again.

He hopped to the door and held it for her. Partly to urge her inside, and partly to catch her if she stumbled. She was seventy-five if she was a day, and despite her high energy and general bossiness, he felt protective.

Not that he'd be much help if she fell, with this broken leg.

She rolled her eyes and walked inside, shaking her head.

When he turned back, Angelica was about ten feet away from the front porch. She'd stopped and was watching him. Eyes huge, wide, wary. From here, he could see the dark circles under them.

Unwanted concern nudged at him. She looked as though she hadn't slept, hadn't been eating right. Her clothes were worn, suggesting poverty. And the flirty sparkle in her eyes, the one that had kept all the farm boys buying gallons of lemonade from her concession stand at the county fair…that was completely gone.

She looked defeated. At the end of her rope.

What had happened to her?

Their mutual sizing-up stare-fest lasted way too long, and then he beckoned her forward. "Come on up. I'm afraid I can't greet you properly with this bum leg."

She trotted up the stairs, belying his impression that she was beaten down. "Was that Lou Ann Miller?"

"It was." He felt an illogical urge to step closer to her, which he ascribed to the fact that he didn't get out much and didn't meet many women. "She runs my life."

"Miss Lou Ann!" Angelica called through the screen door, seemingly determined to ignore Troy. "Haven't seen you in ages!"

Lou Ann, who must have been directly inside, hurried back out.

Angelica's face broke into a smile as she pulled the older woman into a gentle hug. "It's so nice to see you! How's Caleb?"

Troy drummed his fingers on the handle of his crutch. Caleb was Lou Ann's grandson, who'd been in Angelica's grade in school, and whom Angelica had dated before the two of them had gotten together. He was just one of the many members of Angelica's fan club back then, and Troy, with his young-guy pride and testosterone, had been crazy jealous of all of them.

Maybe with good reason.

"He's fine, fine. Got two young boys." Lou Ann held Angelica's shoulders and studied her. "You're way too thin. I'll bring out some cookies." She glared at Troy. "They're not for you, so don't you go eating all of them."

And then she was gone and it was just the two of them.

* * *

Angelica studied the man she'd been so madly in love with seven years ago.

He was as handsome as ever, despite the cast on his leg and the two-day ragged beard on his chin. His shoulders were still impossibly broad, but now there were tiny wrinkles beside his eyes, and his short haircut didn't conceal the fact that his hairline was a little higher than it used to be. The hand he held out to her was huge.

Angelica's stomach knotted, but she forced herself to reach out and put her hand into his.

The hard-calloused palm engulfed hers and she yanked her hand back, feeling trapped. She squatted down to pet the grizzled bulldog at Troy's side. "Who's this?"

"That's Bull."

She blinked. Was he calling her on her skittishness?

That impression increased as he cocked his head to one side. "You're not afraid of me, are you?"

"No!" She gulped air. "I'm not afraid of you. Like I said when we texted, I'm here to apply for the job you advertised in the *Tribune*."

He gestured toward one of the rockers. "Have a seat. Let's talk about that. I'm curious about why you're interested."

Of course he was. And she'd spent much of last night sleepless, wondering how much she'd have to tell him to get the job she desperately needed, the job that would make things as good as they could be, at least for a while.

Once she sat down, he made his way back to his own rocker and sat, grimacing as he propped his leg on the low table in front of him.

She didn't like the rush of sympathy she felt. "What happened?"

"Fell off a roof. My own stupid fault."

That was new in him, the willingness to admit his own culpability. She wondered how far it went.

"That's why I need an assistant with the dogs," he explained. "Lou Ann helps me around the house, but she's not strong enough to take care of the kennels. I can't get everything done, and we've got a lot of dogs right now, so this is kind of urgent."

His words were perfectly cordial, but questions and undercurrents rustled beneath them.

Angelica forced herself to stay in the present, in sales mode. "You saw my résumé online, right? I worked as a vet assistant back in Boston. And I've done hospital, um, volunteer work, and you know I grew up in the country. I'm strong, a lot stronger than I look."

He nodded. "I've no doubt you could do the work if you wanted to," he said, "but why would you want to?"

"Let's just say I need a job."

He studied her, his blue eyes troubled. "You haven't shown your face in town for seven years. Even when you visit your grandfather, you hide out at the Senior Towers. If I'm giving you access to my dogs and my computer files and my whole business, especially if you're able to live here on the grounds, I need to know a little more about what you've been up to."

He hadn't mentioned his main reason for mistrusting her, and she appreciated that. She pulled her mind out of the past and focused on the living arrangement, one of the main reasons this job was perfect for her. "I'm very interested in living in. Your ad said that's part of the job?"

"That's right, in the old bunkhouse." He gestured

toward a trim white building off to the east. "I figured the offer of housing might sweeten the deal, given that this is just a temporary job."

"Is it big enough for two?"

"Ye-es," He leaned back in the rocker and studied her, his eyes hooded. "Why? Are you married? I thought your name was still Camden."

"I'm not married." She swallowed. "But I do have a son."

His eyebrows lifted. "How old is your son?"

"Is that important?" She really, really didn't want to tell him.

"Yes, it's important," he said with a slight sigh. "I can't have a baby or toddler here. It wouldn't be safe, not with some of the dogs I care for."

She drew in a breath. Now or never. "My son's six, almost seven." She reached a hand out to the bulldog, who'd settled between them, rubbed it along his wrinkled head, let him sloppily lick her fingers.

"Six! Then…"

She forced herself to look at Troy steadily while he did the math. Saw his eyes harden as he realized her son must have been conceived right around the time she'd left town.

Heat rose in her cheeks as the familiar feeling of shame twisted her insides. But she couldn't let herself go there. "Xavier is a well-behaved kid." At least most of the time. "He loves animals and he's gentle with them."

Troy was still frowning.

He was going to refuse her, angry about the way she'd left him, and then what would she do? How would she achieve the goal she'd set for herself, to fulfill as many of Xavier's wishes as she could? This was such a perfect arrangement.

"I really need this job, Troy." She hated to beg, but for Xavier, she'd do it.

He looked away, out at the fields, and she did, too. Sun on late-summer corn tassels, puffy clouds in a blue sky. Xavier would love it so.

"If you ever felt anything for me…" Her throat tightened and she had to force out the words. "If any of your memories about me are good, please give me the job."

He turned back toward her, eyes narrowing. "Why do you need it so badly?"

She clenched her hands in her lap. "Because my son wants to be close to Gramps. And because he loves animals."

"Most people don't organize their careers around their kids' hankerings."

She drew in a breath. "Well, I do."

His expression softened a little. "This job…it might not be what you want. It's just until my leg heals. The doc says it could be three, four months before I'm fully back on my feet. Once that happens, I won't need an assistant anymore."

She swallowed and squeezed her hands together. *Lord, I know I'm supposed to let You lead, but this seems so right. Not for me, but for Xavier, and that's what matters. It is of You, isn't it?*

No answer from above, but the roar of a truck engine pierced the country quiet.

Oh no. Gramps was back too soon. He'd never gotten along with Troy, never trusted him on account of his conflicts with Troy's dad. But she didn't want the two men's animosity to get in the way of what both she and her son wanted and needed.

The truck stopped again at the end of the driveway. Gramps got out, walked around to the passenger door.

She surged from her chair. "No, don't!" she called, but the old man didn't hear her. She started down the porch steps

Troy called her back. "It's okay, they can come up. Regardless of what we decide about the job, maybe your son would like to see the dogs, look around the place."

"There's nothing he'd like better," she said, "but I don't want to get his hopes up if this isn't going to work out."

Troy's forehead wrinkled as he stared out toward the truck, watching as Gramps helped Xavier climb out.

Angelica rarely saw her son from this distance, and now, watching Gramps steady him, her hand rose to her throat. He looked as thin as a scarecrow. His baseball cap couldn't conceal the fact that he had almost no hair.

Her eyes stung and her breathing quickened as if she were hyperventilating. She pinched the skin on the back of her hand, hard, and pressed her lips together.

Gramps held Xavier's arm as they made slow progress down the driveway. The older supporting the younger, opposite of how it should be.

Troy cleared his throat. "Like I said, the job won't be long-term. I…it looks like you and your son have some…issues. You might want to find something more permanent."

His kind tone made her want to curl up and cry for a couple of weeks, but she couldn't go there. She clenched her fists. "I know the job is short-term." Swallowing the lump that rose in her throat, she added, "That's okay with us. We take things a day at a time."

"Why's that?" His gaze remained on the pair making their slow way up the driveway.

He was going to make her say it. She took a shuddering breath and forced out the words. "Because the doctors aren't sure how long his remission will last."

Troy stared at Xavier, forgetting to breathe. Remission? "Remission from what?"

Angelica cleared her throat. "Leukemia. He has…a kind that's hard to beat."

Every parent's nightmare. Instinctively he reached out to pat her shoulder, the way he'd done so many times with pet owners worried about seriously ill pets.

She flinched and sidled away.

Fine! Anger flared up at the rejection and he gripped the porch railing and tamped it down. Her response was crystal clear. She didn't want any physical contact between them.

But no matter his own feelings, no matter what Angelica had done to him, the past was the past. This pain, the pain of a mother who might lose her child, was in the present, and Angelica's worn-down appearance suddenly made sense.

And no matter whose kid Xavier was…no matter who she'd cheated on him with…the boy was an innocent, and the thought of a child seriously, maybe terminally, ill made Troy's heart hurt.

Again he suppressed his emotions as his medical instincts went into overdrive. "What kind of doctors has he seen? Have you gotten good treatments, second opinions?"

She took a step back and crossed her arms over her chest. "I can't begin to tell you how many doctors and opinions."

"But are they the best ones? Have you tried the Cleveland—"

"Troy!" She blew out a jagged breath. "Look, I don't need medical interference right now. I need a job."

"But—"

"Don't you think I've done everything in my power to help him?" She turned away and walked down the steps toward her son. Her back was stiff, her shoulders rigid.

He lifted a hand to stop her and then let it fall. *Way to go, Hinton. Great social skills.*

He'd find out more, would try to do something to help. Obviously Angelica hadn't done well financially since she left him and left town. Xavier's father must have bolted. And without financial resources, getting good medical care wasn't easy.

"Mom! Did you get the job?"

Angelica shot Troy a quick glance. "It's still being decided."

The boy's face fell. Then he nodded and bit his lip. "It's okay, Mama. But can we at least see the dogs?"

"Absolutely," Troy answered before Angelica could deny the boy. Then he hobbled down the porch stairs and sank onto the bottom one, putting him on a level with the six-year-old. "I'm Troy," he said, and reached out to shake the boy's hand.

The boy smiled—wow, what a smile—and reached out to grasp Troy's hand, looking up at his mother for reassurance.

She nodded at him. "You know what to say."

Frowning with thought, the boy shook his head.

"Pleased to…" Angelica prompted.

The smile broke out again like sunshine. "Oh yeah. Pleased to meet you, sir. I'm Xavier." He dropped Troy's hand and waved an arm upward, grinning. "And this is my grandpa. My *great*-grandpa."

"I've already had the pleasure." Troy looked up and met the old man's hostile eyes.

Camden glared down at him, not speaking.

Oh man. Out of the gazillion reasons not to hire Angelica, here was a major one. Obviously her grandfather was an important part of her life, one of her only living relatives. If she and Xavier came to live here, Troy would see a lot of Homer Camden, something they'd managed to avoid for the years Angelica was out of town.

Of course, he'd been working like crazy himself. Setting up his private practice, opening the rescue, paying off debt from vet school, which was astronomical even though his family had helped.

Troy pushed himself to his feet and got his crutches underneath him. "Dogs are out this way, if you'd like to see them." He nodded toward the barn.

"Yes!" Xavier pumped his arm. "I asked God to get me a bunch of dogs."

"Zavey Davey..." Angelica's voice was uneasy. "Remember, I don't have the job yet. And God doesn't always—"

"I know." Xavier sighed, his smile fading a little. "He doesn't always answer prayers the way we want Him to."

Ouch. Kids were supposed to be all about Jesus Loves Me and complete confidence in God's—and their parents'—ability to fix anything. But from the looks of things, young Xavier had already run up against some of life's hard truths.

"Come on, Gramps." When the old man didn't move, Xavier tugged at his arm. "You promised you'd be nice. Please?"

The old man's face reddened. After a slight pause

that gave Troy and Angelica the chance to glance at each other, he turned in the direction Troy had indicated and started walking, slowly, with Xavier.

Angelica touched Troy's arm, more like hit him, actually. "Don't let him go back there if you don't want to give me the job," she growled.

Even angry, her voice brushed at his nerve endings like rich, soft velvet. Her rough touch plucked at some wildness in him he'd never given way to.

Troy looked off over the cornfields, thinking, trying to get control of himself. He didn't trust Angelica, but that sweet-eyed kid…how could he disappoint a sick kid?

Homer Camden and the boy were making tracks toward the barn, and Troy started after them. He didn't want them to reach the dogs before he'd had a chance to lay some ground rules about safety. He turned to make sure Angelica was following.

She wasn't. "Well?" Her arms were crossed, eyes narrowed, head cocked to one side.

"You expect me to make an instant decision?"

"Since my kid's feelings are on the line…yeah. Yeah, I do."

Their eyes locked. Some kind of stormy electrical current ran between them.

This was bad. Working with her would be difficult enough, since feelings he thought he'd resolved years ago were resurfacing. He'd thought he was over her dumping him, but the knowledge that she'd conceived a child with someone else after seeming so sincere about their decision to wait until marriage… His neck felt as tight as granite. Yeah. It was going to take a while to process that.

Having her live here on the grounds with that very

child, someone else's child, the product of her unfaith-fulness…he clenched his jaw against all the things he wanted to say to her.

Fools vent their anger, but the wise hold it back. It was a proverb he'd recently taught the boys in his Kennel Kids group, little dreaming how soon and how badly he'd need it himself.

"Mom! Come on! I wanna see the dogs!" Xavier was tugging at his grandfather's arm, jumping around like a kid who wasn't at all sick, but Troy knew that was deceptive. Even terminally ill animals went through energetic periods.

Could he deprive Xavier of being with dogs and of having a decent home to live in? Even if having Angelica here on the farm was going to be difficult?

When he met her eyes again, he saw that hers shone with unshed tears.

"Okay," he said around a sigh. "You're hired."

Her face broke into a sunshiny smile that reminded him of the girl she'd been. "Thank you, Troy," she said softly. She walked toward him, and for a minute he thought she was going to hug him, as she'd been so quick to do in the past.

But she walked right by him to catch up with her son and grandfather. She bent over, embraced Xavier from behind and spoke into his ear.

The boy let out a cheer. "Way to go, Mama! Come on!"

They hurried ahead, leaving Troy to hop along on his crutches, matching Angelica's grandfather's slower pace.

"Guess you hired her," the old man said.

"I did."

"Now you listen here." Camden stopped walking,

narrowed his eyes, and pointed a finger at Troy. "If you do anything to hurt that girl, you'll have me to contend with."

Troy took a deep breath and let it out slowly. He was doing this family a favor, but he couldn't expect gratitude, not with the history that stood between them. "I have no plans to hurt her. Hoping she'll be a help to me until I'm back on my feet." He glanced down. "Foot."

"Humph." Camden turned and started making his way toward the barn again. "Heard you fell off a roof. Fool thing to do."

Troy gritted his teeth and swung into step beside Camden. "According to my brother and dad, you've done a few fool things in your day." This was a man who'd repeatedly refused a massive financial package that would have turned his family's lives around, all in favor of keeping his single-acre farm that stood in the middle of the Hinton holdings.

Not that Troy blamed the old man, particularly. Troy's father was an arrogant, unstable man with plenty of enemies. Including Troy himself, most of the time.

Even after Homer Camden's health had declined, forcing him to move into the Senior Towers, he clung stubbornly to the land. Rumor had it that his house had fallen into disrepair and the surrounding fields were nothing but weeds.

Not wanting to say something he'd regret, Troy motored ahead on his crutches until he reached Xavier and Angelica, who'd stopped at the gate.

"If you wait there," he said to them, "I'll let the dogs out into the runs." The breeze kicked up just as he passed Angelica, and the strawberry scent of her hair took him back seven years, to a time when that smell and her gentle, affectionate kisses had made him light-headed on a regular basis.

"Wait. Mr. Hinton." Xavier was breathing hard. "Thank you…for giving Mama…the job." He smiled up at Troy.

Troy's throat constricted. "Thank you for talking her into doing it," he managed to say, and then swung toward the barn.

He was going to do everything in his power to make that boy well.

Inside, joyful barks and slobbery kisses grounded him. His dogs ranged in age and size but tended toward the large, dark-coated bully breeds. The dogs no one else wanted to take a risk with: pit bulls, aggressive Dobermans and Rotties, large mutts. They were mixed in with older, sicker dogs whose owners couldn't or wouldn't pay the vet bills to treat them.

He moved among them, grateful that he'd found his calling in life.

Yes, he was lonely. Yes, he regretted not having a family around him, people to love. But he had his work, and it would always be there. Unlike people, dogs were loyal and trustworthy. They wouldn't let you down.

He opened the kennel doors to let them run free.

When he got back outside, he heard the end of Homer Camden's speech. "There's a job might open up at the café," he was saying, "And Jeannette Haroldson needs a caregiver."

For some reason that went beyond his own need for a temporary assistant, Troy didn't want the old man to talk her out of working for him. "Look, I know you've got a beef with the Hintons. But it's my dad and my brother who manage the land holdings. My sister's not involved, and I just run my rescue."

"That's as may be, but blood runs true. Angie's got other choices, and I don't see why—"

"That's why, Grandpa." Angelica pointed to Xavier. He'd knelt down beside the fence, letting the dogs lick him through it. On his face was an expression of the purest ecstasy Troy had ever seen.

All three adults looked at each other. They were three people at odds. But in that moment, in complete silence, a pact arose between them: whatever it takes, we'll put this child first and help him be happy.

Chapter Two

Angelica watched her son reach thin, bluish fingers in to touch the dogs. Listened to Troy lecture them all about the rules for safety: don't enter the pens without a trained person there, don't let the dogs out, don't feed one dog in the presence of others. Her half-broken heart sang with gratitude.

Thanks to God, and Troy, Xavier would have his heartfelt wish. He'd have dogs—multiple dogs—to spend his days with. He'd have a place to call home. He'd have everything she could provide for him to make his time on this earth happy.

And if Xavier was happy, she could handle anything: Troy's intensity, the questions in his eyes, the leap in her own heart that came from being near this too-handsome man who had never been far from her thoughts in all these years.

"Do you want to see the inside of the barn?" Troy asked Xavier.

"Sure!" He sounded livelier than he had in weeks.

Troy led the way, his shoulders working the crutches. He was such a big man; he'd probably had to get the extra-tall size.

Gramps patted her back, stopping her. "I don't like it," he said, "but I understand what you're doing."

She draped an arm around his shoulders. "Thanks. That means a lot."

"Think I'll wait in the truck, though," he said. "Being around a Hinton sticks in my craw."

"Okay, sure." Truthfully, she was glad to see Gramps go. She doubted that he and Troy could be civil much longer.

She held Xavier's hand as they walked into the barn and over to the dog pens. The place was pretty clean, considering. Troy must have been wearing himself out to keep it that way.

As Xavier and Troy played with the dogs, she looked around, trying to get a clue into the man. She wandered over to a desk in the corner, obviously a place where he did the kennel business, or some of it.

And there, among a jumble of nails and paper clips, was a leather-studded bracelet she hadn't seen in seven years. She sucked in a breath as her heart dove down, down, down.

She closed her eyes hard, trying to shut out the memories, but a slide show of them raced through her mind. First date, whirlwind courtship and the most romantic marriage proposal a girl from her background could have imagined. For a few months, she'd felt like a princess in a fairy tale.

Back then, as an engaged couple, they'd helped with the youth group and had gotten the kids True Love Waits bracelets—leather and studs for the guys, more delicate chains for the girls. There had been a couple of extra ones, and one night when the waiting had been difficult, she and Troy had decided to each wear one as a reminder.

Carefully, she picked up the leather band. Her eyes filled with tears as she remembered stroking it on his arm, sometimes jokingly tugging at it when their kisses had gotten too passionate. Back in those innocent, happy days.

She'd ripped hers off and thrown it away on the most awful night of her life. The night she'd turned twenty-one and stupidly gone out with a bunch of friends to celebrate. The night she'd had too much to drink, realized it and accepted the offer of an older acquaintance to walk her home.

The night her purity and innocence and dreams of waiting for marriage had been torn forcibly away.

The next day, when Troy had noticed her bracelet was missing, she'd lied to him, telling him it must have fallen off.

But he'd continued to wear his, joking that he probably needed the reminder more than she did.

"Hey." He came up behind her now. When he noticed what she was holding, his eyebrows shot up and he took a step back.

She dropped it as if it were made of hot metal. "I'm sorry. That's not my business. I just happened to see it and…got carried away with the memories."

He nodded, pressed his lips together. Turned away.

That set face had to be judging her, didn't it? Feeling disgust at her lack of purity.

She'd been right to leave him. He could never have accepted her after what happened, although knowing him, he'd have tried to pretend. He'd have felt obligated to marry her anyway.

"Mom! Come see!" Xavier cried.

"Xavier!" He'd gone into a section of the barn Troy

had warned them was off-limits. "I'm sorry," she said to Troy, and hurried over to her son. "You have to follow the rules! You could get hurt!"

"But look, Mama!" He knelt in front of a small heap of puppies, mostly gray and white, all squirming around a mother who lay on her side. Her head was lifted, her teeth bared.

"Careful of a mama dog," Troy said behind her. "Pull him back a foot or two, will you, Angelica? These little guys are only two weeks old, and the mom's still pretty protective."

She did, hating the crestfallen expression on Xavier's face. This ideal situation might have its own risks.

And then Troy reached down, patted the mother dog and carefully lifted a tiny, squirming puppy into Xavier's lap.

Xavier froze, then put his face down to nuzzle the puppy's pink-and-white snout. It nudged and licked him back, and then two more puppies crawled into his lap, tumbling over each other. Yips and squeals came from the mass of warm puppy bodies.

"Mom," Xavier said reverently. "This is *so* cool."

Angelica's heart did a funny little twist. She reached out and squeezed Troy's arm before she could stop herself.

"Do we really get to live here? Can we sleep in the barn with the puppies?"

Troy laughed. "No, son. You'll stay in a bunkhouse. Kind of like an Old West cowboy. Want to see?"

"Sure!" His eyes were on Troy with something like hero worship, and worry pricked at Angelica's chest. Was Xavier going to get too attached to Troy?

Then again, if it would make him happy… Angelica swallowed hard and shut out thoughts of the future. "Let's go!" she said with a voice that was only slightly shaky.

When they reached the bunkhouse and walked inside, Angelica felt her face break out into a smile. "It's wonderful, Troy! When did you do all this work on it?" She remembered the place as an old, run-down outbuilding, but now modern paneling and new windows made it bright with sunshine on wood. It needed curtains, maybe blue-and-white gingham. The rough-hewn pine furniture was sparse, but with a few throw pillows and afghans, the place would be downright homey.

A home. She'd wanted one forever, and even more after she'd become a mom.

Troy's watchful eyes snapped her out of her happy fantasies. "You like it?"

"It's fantastic." She realized he'd never answered her question about when he'd done the work.

"You're easy to please." His voice was gruff.

She smiled and squatted down beside Xavier. "We both are. Pretty near perfect, isn't it, Zavey Davey?"

"Yes. Sure, Mama."

Her ear was so attuned to his needs that she heard the slight hesitation in his voice. "What's wrong?" she asked, keeping her voice low to make the conversation private, just between her and her son. "Isn't this everything you've always wanted?"

"Yes. Except…" He wrinkled his freckled nose as though he was trying to decide something.

"What? What is it, honey?"

He pressed his lips together and then lost the battle with himself, shrugged and grinned winningly at her. "It's the last thing on my list, Mama."

The last thing. Her heart twisted tight. "What? What do you need?"

He leaned over and whispered into her ear, "A dad."

When Angelica emerged from the bunkhouse the next Saturday, every nerve in Troy's body snapped to attention. Was this the same woman who'd been working like a ranch hand this week, wearing jeans and T-shirts and boots, learning the ropes in the kennel?

It was the first time he'd seen her in a top that wasn't as loose as a sack. And was that makeup on her eyes, making them look even bigger?

"What?" she asked as she walked up beside him. She seemed taller. He looked down and saw that she was wearing sandals with a little heel, too.

Angelica had always been cute and appealing. But now she was model-thin, and with her hair braided back, her cheekbones stood out in a heart-shaped face set off by long silver earrings. A pale pink shirt edged with lace made her copper-colored skin glow. With depth and wisdom in her brown eyes, and a wry smile turning up the edges of her mouth, she was a knockout.

And one he needed to steer clear of. Beauty didn't equate to morality or good values, and one whirl with this little enchantress had just about done him in.

Though to be fair, he didn't know the rest of her story. And he shouldn't judge. "Nothing. You look nice."

"Do you have the keys?"

"What?"

"Keys." She held out her hand.

He had to stop staring. The keys. He pulled them out of his pocket and handed them over.

She wasn't here for him. She was here because she

needed something, and when she got it, she'd leave. He knew that from experience.

"Bye, Mama!" Xavier's voice was thin, reedy, but for all that, cheerful.

When he turned, he saw Xavier and Lou Ann standing on the porch, waving.

"You be good for Miss Lou Ann." Angelica shook her finger at Xavier, giving him a mock-stern look.

"I will, Mama."

Lou Ann put an arm around the boy. "We'll have fun. He's going to help me do some baking."

"Thank you!" Angelica shot a beaming smile toward the porch, and Troy's heart melted a little more.

With him, though, she was all business. "Let's get going. If we're to get there by nine, we don't have time to stand around."

She walked toward the truck, and he couldn't help noticing how well her jeans fit her slender frame.

Then she opened the passenger door and held it for him.

He gritted his teeth. Out of all the indignities of being injured, this had to be the worst. He liked to drive, liked to be in control, liked to open the door for a lady. Not have the door held for him. That was a man's proper role, pounded into him from childhood. No weakness; no vulnerability. Men should be in charge.

While his years in college and vet school, surrounded by capable and brilliant professional women, had knocked some feminist sense into his head, his alpha-male instincts were as strong as ever.

"You need help getting in?" she asked.

Grrrr. "I have a broken leg. I'm not paralyzed." He swung himself into the truck, grunting with the awkward effort.

"Sor-ry." She shrugged and walked back around to the driver's side.

When they headed down the driveway, he said, "Take a right up there at the stop sign."

She did, rolling down her window at the same time. Hot, dusty July air blew tendrils of her hair loose, but she put her head back and breathed it in deeply, a tiny smile curving her full lips.

He liked that she'd stayed a farm girl, not all prissy and citified. Maybe liked it a little too much. "Slow down, this is a blind curve. Then go left after that barn."

"Troy." She shifted gears with complete competence. "I grew up here, remember? I know how to get to town."

Of course she did. She was a capable assistant…and no more. He needed to focus on his weekly vet clinic and how he was going to manage it on crutches. Forget about Angelica.

Easier said than done.

Angelica turned down the lane that led into town, trying to pay attention to the country air blowing through the truck's open windows rather than on the man beside her. He'd been staring at her nonstop since she came outside today. She already felt self-conscious, all dolled up, and Troy's attitude made it worse. She wasn't sure if he was judging her or…something else, but his gaze made her feel overheated, uncomfortable.

Or maybe the problem was that she'd dressed up on purpose, with the notion of finding a dad—or a temporary stand-in for one—to fulfill Xavier's wish. The thought of putting herself out there for men to approach made her feel slightly ill; dating was the last thing she wanted to do. And it wasn't likely that anyone would want damaged goods like her, not likely she'd attract interest, but she had to try. She'd promised herself to make her son's days happy, since she couldn't be sure how many he had left, and she was going to do her best.

Once they reached the residential area that surrounded Rescue River's downtown, Angelica's stomach knotted. Everyone in town knew about what she'd done to Troy, their beloved high school quarterback and brilliant veterinarian and all-around good guy. No doubt her own reputation was in the gutter.

There was the town's famous sign, dating back to Civil War years when the tiny farm community had been home to several safe houses on the Underground Railroad:

Rescue River, Ohio.

All Are Welcome, All Are Safe.

Funny, she didn't feel so safe now. She cruised past the bank and the feed store, and then thoughts of herself vanished when she saw the line of people snaking around the building that housed Troy's veterinary practice. "Wow. Looks like your clinic is a success."

"Lots of people struggling these days."

"It's free?"

He nodded, pointed. "Park right in front. They always save me a place."

She noticed a few familiar faces turning toward their truck. Someone ran to take a lawn chair out of the single remaining parking spot and she pulled in, stopped and went around to see if Troy needed help getting out. But he'd already hopped down, so she grabbed his crutches out of the back and took them to him.

"Here." She handed him the crutches, and his large, calloused hand brushed hers.

Something fluttered inside her chest. She yanked her hand back, dropping a crutch in the process.

"Hey, that you, Angie? Little Angie?"

She turned to see a tall, skinny man, his thin hair pulled back in a ponytail, his face stubbly. She cocked her head to one side. "Derek? Derek Moseley?"

"It *is* you!" He flung an easy arm around her and she shrugged away, and then suddenly Troy was there, stepping between them. "Whoa, my friend," he said. "Easy on my assistant."

"I'm fine!" She took another sidestep away.

Derek lifted his hands like stop signs. "Just saying hi to my old buddy's little sister, Doc." He turned to Angelica. "Girl, I ain't seen you in ages. How's your brother?"

She shook her head. "I don't see him much myself. He's overseas, doing mission work."

"Carlo? A missionary?"

"Well, something like that." In reality, her brother, Carlo, was halfway between a missionary and a mercenary, taking the word of God to people in remote areas where he was as likely to be met with a machete as a welcome.

"Carlo's a great guy. Tell him I said hello."

"I will." That evaluation was spot-on—her brother was a great guy. Carlo was the one who'd gone to Gramps and told him he had to take her in when their parents' behavior had gone way out of control. He'd been sixteen; she'd been nine. He'd gone out on his own then, had his dark and dangerous times, but now he'd found Jesus and reformed. He wrote often, sent money even though she told him not to, probably more than he could afford. But she didn't see him enough and she wished he'd come home. Especially now, with Xavier's health so bad.

A shuffling sound broke into her consciousness. She looked around for Troy and saw him working his way toward the clinic on his crutches, large medical bag clutched awkwardly at his side.

She hurried to him. "Here, let me carry that."

"I can get it."

Stepping in front of him, she took hold of the bag. "Probably, but not very well. This is what you're paying me for."

He held on to the bag a second longer and then let it go. "Fine."

As they walked toward the clinic, people greeted Troy, thanked him for being there, asked about his leg. The line seemed endless. Most people held dogs on leads, but a few had cat carriers. One man sat on a bench beside an open-topped cardboard box holding a chicken.

How would Troy ever take care of all these people? "The clinic's only until noon, right? Do you have help?"

"A vet tech, whenever he gets here. And I stay until I've seen everyone. We work hard. You up for this?"

She was and they did work hard; he wasn't lying. The morning flew by with pet after pet. She held leashes for Pomeranians and pit bulls, got scratched by a frightened tomcat with a ripped ear and comforted a twenty-something girl who cried when her two fluffy fur-ball puppies, one black and one white, had to get shots. She wrote down the particulars of rescue situations people told Troy about. Dogs needed rabies shots and ear medicine, X-rays and spaying. If it was something he couldn't do right at the moment, he made a plan to do it later in the week.

She asked once, "Can you even do surgery, with your leg?"

"My leg doesn't hurt as much as that guy's hurting," he said, scratching the droopy ears of a basset-beagle mix with a swollen stomach. The owner was pretty sure he'd swallowed a baby's Binky. "Feed him canned pumpkin to help things along," he told the owner. "If he doesn't pass it within three days, or if he's in more pain, call me."

A fiftysomething lady came in with a small, scruffy white dog wrapped in a towel. "Afraid he's got to be put to sleep, Doc." Her voice broke as she lifted the skinny animal to the metal exam table.

Angelica moved closer and patted the woman's back, feeling completely ineffectual. She wanted to help, but sometimes there wasn't anything you could do.

"Let's not jump to that conclusion." Troy picked up the whimpering little creature, ignoring its feeble effort to bite at him. He felt carefully around the dog's abdomen and examined its eyes and ears. "I'm guessing pancreatitis," he said finally, "but we'll need to do some blood work to be sure."

"What's that mean, Doc?" the woman asked. "I don't have much extra money…and I don't want him to suffer." She buried her face in her hands.

Angelica's throat ached. She could identify. She found a box of tissues and brought it over.

"Hey." Troy put a hand on the woman's shoulder. "Let's give treatment a try. If you can't afford the medicine, we'll work something out."

"Is he even likely to live?"

"Fifty-fifty," Troy admitted. "But I'm not a quitter. We can bring the dog to the farm if you don't have time to do the treatments. Aren't you a night waitress out at the truck stop?"

She nodded. "That's the other thing. I can't stick around home to care for him. I gotta work to pay my rent."

"Let me take him to the farm, then," Troy said. "It's

worth it. He may have years of running around left. Don't you want me to try?"

"You'd really do that for him?" Hope lit the woman's face as she carefully picked up the little dog and cradled him to her chest. When she looked up, her eyes shone. "You don't know how much this means to me, Doc. He's been with me through two divorces and losing my day job and a bout with cancer. I want to be able to give back to him. I'll donate all my tips when I get them."

"Give what you can. That's all I ask." He told Angelica what to do next and took the dog away.

A man in jeans and a scrub top strode into the clinic then, and Angelica studied him as he greeted Troy. He must be the vet tech they'd been waiting for.

"Buck," Troy said. "How goes it?"

Buck. So that was why he looked so familiar—he was an old classmate, one of the nicer boys. "Hey," she greeted him. "Remember me?"

"Is that you, Angie?" A smile lit his eyes. "Haven't seen you in forever. How's your grandpa?"

They chatted for a few minutes while Troy entered data into a computer, preparing for the next appointment. Buck kept smiling and stepped a little closer, and Angelica recognized what was happening: he *like* liked her, as her girlfriends back in Boston would say. She took a step away.

And then it dawned on her: Buck would be a perfect guy to help fulfill Xavier's dream. Oh, not to marry, she couldn't go that far, but if she could find a nice, harmless man to hang out with some in the evenings, watch some family shows with, play board games with…that didn't sound half-bad. Xavier would be thrilled.

Come on, flirt with the man. You used to be good at it.

But she barely remembered how to talk to a man that way. And anyway, it felt like lying. How could she pretend to have an interest in a nice guy like Buck just to make her son happy? Maybe this wasn't such a good plan after all.

When Troy came back, ready for the next patient, Buck cocked his head to one side. "Are you two together? I remember you used to—"

"No!" they both said at the same time.

"Whoa, okay! I just thought you were engaged, back in the day."

Angelica felt her face heat. "I'm just his assistant while he gets back on his feet," she explained as the next patient came in.

"Glad to hear you've come to your senses about him," Buck joked.

Troy's lips tightened and he turned away, limping over to greet a couple with a cat carrier who'd just walked in.

"You back in town for a while?" Buck looked at Angelica with sharpened interest.

"Yes. For a…a little while."

"Long enough to have dinner with an old friend?"

He was asking her out. To dinner, and really, what would be the harm? This was what she wanted.

"Sure," she said. "I'll have dinner with you."

"Saturday night? Where are you staying?" He touched her shoulder to usher her over to the side of the exam area, and she forced herself not to pull away.

They agreed on a time and exchanged phones to punch in numbers.

When she looked up, Troy was watching them, eyes narrowed, jaw set.

She shook her hair back. There was no reason for

him to feel possessive. What had been between them was long gone.

So why did she feel so guilty?

Chapter Three

By the time they'd gotten back to the farm, it was suppertime and Troy's blood was boiling as hot as the pot of pasta on the stove.

Did Angelica have to make her date plans right in front of him? And with Buck Armstrong?

But it wasn't his business, and he had no reason to care. He just needed some time to himself.

Which apparently he wasn't going to get, because the minute they set down their things, Xavier was pulling at his hand. "Mr. Troy, Mr. Troy, we're all going to have dinner together!"

Great. He smiled down at the boy. How was he going to get out of this?

"Xavier, honey." Angelica knelt down beside her son. "We'll have dinner at the bunkhouse. We can't impose."

She tugged the ponytail holder out of her hair, and the shiny locks flowed down her back. Her hand kneaded Xavier's shoulder. She was all loving mother.

And all woman.

"But, Mama! Wait till you see what Miss Lou Ann and me cooked!"

Lou Ann rubbed Xavier's bald head. "I'm sorry, Angelica. I told him we could probably all eat together. We picked zucchini and tomatoes from the garden and cooked up some of that ratatouille."

"And we made a meat loaf, and I got to mix it up with my hands!"

The boy sounded so happy. Troy's throat tightened as he thought about how Angelica must feel, cherishing every moment with him and wondering at the same time whether he'd ever make meat loaf again, whether this was the last chance for this particular activity.

Angelica glanced up at him, eyebrows raised. "Maybe we'll get together another time. Mr. Troy's been working all day and he's tired. Let's let him rest."

What was he supposed to do now, squash down all of this joy? And he had to admit that the thought of having company for dinner in the farmhouse kitchen didn't sound half-bad, except that the pretty woman opposite him was hankering after another man.

At the thought of Angelica dating Buck Armstrong, something dark twisted his insides. With everything he knew about Buck, he should warn her off, and yet it would serve her right to go out with him and find out what he was really like.

"Can we stay, Mr. Troy?"

He looked at the boy's hopeful eyes. "Of course." His words sounded so grudging that he added, "Sounds like a good meal you fixed."

"It is good, and wait till you see dessert!"

By the time Xavier helped Lou Ann serve dessert— sliced pound cake, topped with berries and whipped cream—he looked beat. But his smile was joyous. "I had so much fun this afternoon, Mama!"

Troy praised the food, which was really good, thanks

he was sure to Lou Ann's guidance. But his stomach was turning, wouldn't let him really enjoy it.

Angelica looked beautiful at the other end of the table, her black hair tumbling down past her shoulders and her cheeks pink as apples. And now, with Xavier so happy, she didn't seem as worried as usual; the little line that tended to live between her eyebrows was gone, and her smile flashed frequently as Xavier described all that he and Lou Ann had done that day.

Troy had always wanted this. He wanted a warm, beautiful woman and cute, enthusiastic children at his table, wanted to be the man of the family. And this sweet, feisty pair seemed to fit right into his home and his heart. But he had to keep reminding himself that this wasn't his and it wouldn't last.

Looking at Xavier, he couldn't believe the child had been so sick and might relapse at any moment. Yeah, he was drooping, getting tired, but he was so full of life that it made no sense that God might take him away.

Any more than it made sense that God would put him and his siblings in a loveless family, let alone give Angelica all the heartaches she'd endured growing up, but that was God for you—making sense wasn't what He was about. That was why Troy had stopped trusting Him, starting taking most things into his own hands. He believed, sure; he just didn't trust. And he sure didn't want to join the men's Bible study his friend Dion was always bugging him about.

"This little one needs to get to bed," Lou Ann said. "Troy, I know you can't carry much with those crutches, but why don't you at least help her with the doors and such?"

"Oh, you don't have to—" Angelica stood, looking

suddenly uncomfortable. "We've already taken too much of your time. We can make it."

But Troy moved to intercept her protest. "Come on, pal. Let's get you out to bed."

Angelica started gathering Xavier's pills and toys and snacks together, stuffing them into a Spider-Man backpack. Before she could bend to pick Xavier up, Troy leaned on one crutch, steadied himself with a hip against the table and picked up the boy himself. He was amazingly light. He nestled right against Troy's chest and Troy felt his heart break a little. He glanced over at Angelica and saw that she had tears in her eyes. "Ready?" he asked. Then, gently, he put her son in her arms, taking the boy's backpack to carry himself.

She bit her lip, turned and headed off, and he grabbed his crutches and followed her. They walked out to the bunkhouse together and Troy helped Angelica lay Xavier in his bed, noticing the homey touches Angelica had put around—a teddy bear, a poster of a baseball player, a hand-knitted afghan in shades of blue and brown. It was a boy's room, and it should be filling up with trophies from Little League games. They said every kid got a trophy these days, and wasn't that awful? But not Xavier. This kid hadn't had the opportunity to play baseball.

Not yet.

Angelica knelt beside the bed. "Let's thank God for today."

"Thank You, God, for letting me cook dinner. And for Lou Ann. And the dogs."

Angelica was holding Xavier's hand. "Thank You for giving us food and love and each other."

"Bless all the people who don't have so much," they said together.

"And, God, please get me a daddy before…" Xavier trailed off, turned over.

Whoa. Troy's throat tightened.

"Night, sweetie, sleep tight." Angelica's voice sounded choked.

"Don't let the bedbugs… Love you, Mama." The words were fading off and the boy was asleep.

They both stood looking down at him, Troy on one side of the bed and Angelica on the other.

"Did he say he wants a…dad?" Troy ventured finally.

Angelica nodded.

"Does his dad ever spend time with him?"

She looked up at him. "No. Never."

"Does he even know him?"

Her lips tightened. "I… Look, Troy, I don't want to talk about that."

"Sure." But he'd like to strangle the guy who'd loved and left her, and not just because he remembered how difficult it had been to keep his hands off Angelica back when they were engaged. He took a deep breath and loosened his tightly clasped fists. She'd gotten pregnant with Xavier right around the time she left town, so was Xavier's dad—the jerk—from here or from elsewhere? She hadn't married him, apparently, but… "If the guy knew Xavier, knew what he was like and what he's facing, surely he'd be willing—"

"No."

"No?"

"Just…no, okay?" She stood and stalked out to the living room, and Troy wondered whether he'd ever stop putting his plaster-covered foot in his mouth around her.

* * *

The next Saturday, Angelica touched up her hair with a curling wand and applied blush and mascara. And tried not to throw up.

She didn't want to go out on a date. But there was no other way to get Xavier off her case.

In fact, he was beside her now, hugging her leg. "You never had a date before, Mama."

She laughed. "Yes, I did. Back in the day. Before you."

"Did you go on dates with my dad?"

All Xavier knew was that his father had died. He hadn't ever asked whether Angelica and his father had been married, and Angelica hoped he didn't go there any time soon. For now, she would stick as close to the truth as possible. "No, not with him, but with a few other guys." She tried to deflect his attention. "Just like I'm doing now. Do I look all right?"

"You're beautiful, Mama."

She hugged him. "Thanks, Zavey Davey. You're kinda cute yourself."

"Do I get to meet him? Because I want to see, you know, if he's the right kind of guy for us."

"My little protector. You can meet him sometime, but not now. Miss Lou Ann is going to come over and play with you. And I think I hear her now."

Sure enough, there was a knock on the bunkhouse door. Xavier ran over to get it while Angelica fussed with herself a little more. She'd much rather just stay home with Xavier tonight. What if Buck tried something? She knew him to be a nice guy, but still…

"Well, how's my little friend for the evening?" Lou Ann asked, pinching Xavier's cheek. "You set up for a

Candy Land marathon, or are we building a fort out of sheets and chairs?"

"You'll build a fort with me?" Xavier's eyes turned worshipful. "Mom always says it's too messy."

"It's only too messy if we don't clean up later. And we will, right?"

"Right. I'll get the extra sheets."

As soon as he was out of the room, Lou Ann turned to Angelica. "You look pretty," she said. "Somebody's already cranky, and when he sees you looking like that…" She smacked her lips. "Sparks are gonna fly."

That was the last thing she needed. Her face heated and she changed the subject. "Xavier can stay up until eight-thirty. He gets his meds and a snack half an hour before bed." She showed Lou Ann the pills and the basket of approved snacks.

"That's easy. Don't worry about us." Lou Ann leaned back and looked out the window. "I think your friend just pulled in."

"I wanna see him!" Xavier rushed toward the window, dropping the stack of sheets he'd been carrying.

"Well," Lou Ann said, "that's just fine, because I want to claim the best spot in the fort."

Xavier spun back to Lou Ann. "I'm king of the fort!"

"You'd better get over here and help me, then."

Thank you, Angelica mouthed to Lou Ann, and slipped out the door.

Buck emerged from his black pickup, looking good from his long jean-clad legs to his slightly shaggy brown curls. Any girl would feel fortunate to be dating such a cute guy, Angelica told herself, trying to lighten the lead weight in her stomach.

He's a nice guy. And it's for Xavier. "Hi there!"

"Well, don't you look pretty!" He walked toward her, loose limbed.

To her right, the front door of the main house opened. Troy. He came out on the porch and stood, arms crossed. For all the world as if he were her father.

She narrowed her eyes at him, trying to ignore his rougher style of handsome, the way his broad shoulders, leaning on his crutches, strained the seams of his shirt. She was through with Troy Hinton, and he was most certainly through with her, wouldn't want anything to do with her if he knew the truth.

She deliberately returned her attention to Buck. He reached her and opened his arms.

Really? Was a big hug normal on a first date? It had been so long…and she'd been so young… She took a deep breath and allowed him to hug her, at the same time wrinkling her nose. Something was wrong…

"Baby, it's great to see you. Man, feels good to hug a woman." Buck's words were slurred. And yes, that smell was alcohol, covered with a whole lot of peppermint.

She tried to pull back, but he didn't let go.

Panic rose in her. She stepped hard onto his foot. "Let go," she said, loud, right in his ear.

From the corner of her eye, the sight of Troy made her feel secure.

"Sorry!" Buck stepped back. "I didn't mean…I was just glad…oh man, you look so good." He moved as though he was going to hug her again.

She sidestepped. "Buck. How much have you had to drink?"

"What?" He put an arm around her and started guiding her toward his truck. "I had a drink before I came over. One drink. Don't get uptight."

Could that be true? Without a doubt, she was uptight around men. But this felt wrong in a different way. "Wait a minute. I...I think we should talk a little bit before we go."

"Sure!" He shifted direction, guiding her toward a bench and plopping down too hard, knocking into her so that she sat down hard, too.

She drew in a breath and let it out in a sigh. He was drunk, all right. It wasn't just her being paranoid. But now, how did she get rid of him?

"I really like you, Angelica," he said, putting an arm around her. He pulled her closer.

She scooted away. "Look, Buck, I can't...I don't think I can go out with you. You've had too much to drink."

"One drink!" He sounded irritated.

Angelica stood and backed away. Couldn't something, just once, be easy? "Sorry, friend, but I can't get in the truck with you. And you shouldn't be driving, either."

There was a sound of booted feet, and then Troy was beside her. "She's right, Buck."

"What you doing here, Hinton?"

"I live here, as you very well know."

"Well, I'm taking this little lady out for a meal, once—"

"You're not going anywhere except home. As soon as your sister gets here to pick you up."

"Oh man, you didn't call Lacey!" Buck staggered to his feet, his hand going to his pocket. He pulled out truck keys. "This has been a bust."

Angelica glanced at Troy, willing him to let her handle it. She had plenty of experience with drunk people, starting with her own parents. "Can I see the car keys a minute?"

He held them out, hope lighting up his face. "You gonna come after all? I'll let you drive."

She took the keys. "I'm not going, and sorry, but you're not fit to drive yourself, either."

He lunged to get them back and Troy stuck out a crutch to trip him. "You're not welcome on this property until you're sober."

Angelica kept backing off while, in the distance, a Jeep made clouds on the dusty road. That must be Buck's sister.

So she could go home now. Back inside. Face Xavier and tell him the date was off.

Except she couldn't, because tears were filling her eyes and blurring her vision. She blinked hard and backed up as far as the porch steps while Troy greeted the woman who'd squealed up in the Jeep.

The woman pushed past Troy, poked a finger in Buck's chest and proceeded to chew him out. Then she and Troy helped him into the passenger seat. They stood beside the Jeep for a minute, talking.

When Angelica turned away, she realized that Xavier could see her here if he looked out the window. Hopefully he was too deep into fort-building to notice, but she wasn't ready to see him and she couldn't take the risk. She headed out to the kennels at a jog. Grabbed one of the pit bulls she'd been working with, a black-and-white beauty named Sheena, attached a leash to her and started walking down the field road as unwanted, annoying tears came faster and faster.

She sank to her knees beside a wooden fence post, willing the tears to stop, hugging the dog that licked her cheek with canine concern.

"Get yourself together, girlie. Nobody said life's a tea party."

Gramps' words, harsh but kindly meant, had guided her through the storms of adolescence and often echoed in her mind.

Today, for some reason, they didn't help. She squeezed her eyes shut and tried to pray, but the tears kept coming.

After long moments, one of the verses she'd memorized during Xavier's treatment came into her mind.

Fear not, for I am with you; be not dismayed, for I am your God; I will strengthen you, I will help you, I will uphold you with My righteous right hand.

Slowly, peace, or at least resignation, started to return. But every time she thought about Xavier and how disappointed he'd be, the tears overflowed again.

A hand gripped her shoulder, making her start violently. "You that upset about Buck?" Troy asked.

She shook her head, fighting for control. It wasn't about Buck, not really. He was a small disappointment in the midst of a lot of big ones, but it was enough to push her over the edge. She couldn't handle the possibility of losing Xavier, the only good thing in her life, and yet she had to handle it. And she had to stay strong and positive for him.

It was pretty much her mantra. She breathed in, breathed out. *Stay strong*, she told herself. *Stay strong*.

A couple of minutes later she was able to accept Troy's outstretched hand and climb to her feet. He took the dog leash from her and handed her an ancient-looking, soft bandanna. "It's not pretty, but it's clean."

She nodded and wiped her eyes and nose and came back into herself enough to be embarrassed at how she must look. She wasn't one of those pretty, leak-a-few-tears criers; she knew her eyes must be red and puffy, and she honked when she blew her nose. "Sorry," she said to him.

"For what?"

She shook her head, and by unspoken agreement they started walking. "Sorry to break down."

"You're entitled."

The sun was setting now, sending pink streaks across the sky, and a slight breeze cooled the air. Crickets harmonized with bullfrogs in a gentle rise and fall. Angelica breathed in air so pungent with hay and summer flowers that she could almost taste it, and slowly the familiar landscape brought her calm.

"You know," Troy ventured after a few minutes, "Buck Armstrong's not really worth all that emotion. Not these days. If I'd known you were this into dating him, I might have warned you he has a drinking problem."

She laughed, and that made her cry a little more, and she wiped her eyes. "It's not really about Buck."

He didn't say anything for a minute. Then he gave her shoulder a gentle squeeze. "You've got a lot on your plate."

"I've got a plan, is what I've got," she said, "and I was hoping Buck could be a part of it." Briefly, she explained her intention of finding a stand-in dad for Xavier.

Troy shook his head. "That's not going to work."

"What do you mean?"

"He's a smart kid. He'll know. You can't just pretend you're dating someone so that he'll think he's getting a dad."

"I can if I want to." They came to a crossroads and she glanced around. "I'm not ready to go back home and admit defeat yet, and I don't want him looking out the window and seeing me cry."

"Come the back way, by the kennel."

Sheena, the dog she'd brought with her, jumped at a squirrel, and Troy let her off the lead to chase it. She romped happily, ears flopping.

"So you think getting a dad will make Xavier happy? Even if it's a fake dad?"

"It's not fake! Or, well, it is, but for a good reason." She reached into her pocket and pulled out the picture she always carried, Xavier in happier times. "Look at that face! For all I know, he'll never be really healthy again." She cleared her throat. "If I can make his life happy, I'm going to do it."

He studied the picture. "He played Little League?"

She swallowed hard around the lump in her throat. "T-ball. He'd just started when he was diagnosed. He had one season."

"He started young."

She nodded. "They let him start a few weeks before his birthday, even though officially they aren't supposed to start until they turn four."

"Because he was sick?"

She shook her head. "Because he was so good. He loved it." Tears rushed to her eyes again and she put her hands to her face.

"Hey." He took the sloppy bandanna from her hand, wiped her eyes and nose as if she were a child, and pulled her to his chest. And for just a minute, after a reflexive flinch, Angelica let herself enjoy the feeling. His chest was broad and strong, and she heard the slow beating of his heart. She aligned her breath with his and it steadied her, calmed her.

In just a minute, she'd back away. Because this was dangerous and it wasn't going anywhere. Troy wouldn't want a woman like Angelica, not really, so letting an attraction build between them was a huge mistake.

* * *

Troy patted Angelica's back and breathed in the strawberry scent of her hair, trying to remind himself why he needed to be careful.

He wanted to help Angelica and Xavier in the worst way. His heart was all in with this little family. But that heart was broken, wounded, not whole.

He felt her stiffen in his arms, as though she was just realizing how close he was. For the thousandth time since he'd reencountered her, he wondered about her skittishness around men. Or was it just around him? No, he'd seen her tense up when Armstrong had hugged her, too.

Carefully, he held her upper arms and stepped away. Her face was blotched and wet, but she still looked beautiful. Her Western-style shirt was unbuttoned down to a modest V, sleeves rolled up to reveal tanned forearms. Her jeans clung to her slim figure. Intricate silver earrings hung from her ears, sparkling against her wavy black hair.

"Come on," he said gruffly, "let's go in the house. We'll get you something to drink."

"Okay." She looked up at him, her eyes vulnerable, and he wanted nothing more than to protect her.

Don't go there, fool.

They walked back along the country road as the last bit of sun set in a golden haze. A few dogs barked out their farewell to the day. At the kennel, they put Sheena back inside, and then he led Angelica up to the house.

He loved his farm, his dogs, his life. He had so much. But what right did he have to be happy when Angelica's problems were so big?

How could he help her?

An idea slammed into him, almost an audible voice.

You could marry her.

Immediately he squelched the notion. Ridiculous. No way. He wouldn't go down that path. Not again, not after what she'd done to him.

And even outside of the way she'd dumped him, he'd never seen a good marriage. He didn't know how to be married; didn't know how to relate to people that way; didn't know how to keep a woman happy or make it last. He didn't want to be like his dad, the person who failed his wife. He didn't want to let Xavier down.

But the point was, he thought as he held the door for her, Xavier might not have the time to be let down. Xavier needed and wanted a dad now, and Troy already knew the boy liked him.

As they walked into the kitchen, he remembered proposing to Angelica the last time. Then he'd been all about wanting to impress her, to sweep her away. He'd hired Samantha Weston, who usually used her small plane for crop dusting, to sky-write his proposal at sunset during an all-town Memorial Day picnic. Angelica had laughed, and cried, and joyously accepted. Her friends had clustered around them, and he'd presented her with a diamond way too big for a new vet with school loans to pay off.

He still had that ring, come to think of it. He'd stuffed it in his sock drawer when she mailed it back to him, and he'd never looked at it again.

It was upstairs right now. He could go and get it. Help her handle this massive challenge life had given her. And Xavier... Boy, did he want to help that kid!

Angelica perched on a kitchen stool and rested her chin in her hands. "I guess the idea of Buck as a pretend husband does seem kinda crazy, when I think about it," she admitted. "Anyway, enough about me. How long has Buck had a drinking problem?"

"Since he lost his wife and child," Troy said. "Not only that, but he served a couple of tours in Afghanistan. Which is why I cut the guy a break and let him work at my weekend clinic. I've offered him a full-time job, too, but only if he'll stay sober for six months first. So far, he hasn't been able to do that."

"That's so sad." She bit her lip. "I hope he's going to be okay tonight. I felt bad, but there was no way I was getting into a truck with him."

"And no way he could be Xavier's pseudodad."

"No."

He cracked open a Pepsi and handed it to her. "Here. Sugar and caffeine. It'll make you feel better."

"Always. Thanks." She swung her feet. "Remember buying me a Coke at the drugstore, that very first time we went out?"

He nodded. "And I remember how you sat there drinking it and explaining to me your dating rules. No kissing until the third date. No parking. No staying out past eleven."

"I know, and it wasn't even Gramps making those rules, it was me. I was so scared of getting myself into the same bad situations that landed my folks in trouble. Plus, my brother told me I should be careful about you. Since you were an older man and all." She smiled up at him through her lashes.

His heart rate shot through the ceiling. "Your brother was protective," he said, trying to keep his voice—and his thoughts—on something other than how pretty she was. One question still nagged at him: if she'd had all those rules, then how had she ended up unmarried and pregnant?

"Xavier really misses my brother. Carlo lived near us in Boston for a while, and he's the one who got Xavier involved in T-ball. He did the whole male influence thing, until he got the call to go overseas." She flashed Troy a smile. "If I keep thinking about Carlo I'll get sad again. Save me, Bull!" She slid off the stool and sat cross-legged on the floor. The old bulldog climbed into her lap, and she leaned down and let him lick her face.

"Whoa, Bull, be a gentleman! She'll pass out from your breath!" But he couldn't help enjoying Angelica's affectionate attitude toward his dog. A lot of women didn't want a smelly old dog anywhere around their stockings and fancy dresses, but Angelica was a blue-jeans girl from way back.

He sank down beside her, petting Bull. "So, what are you going to do now? About your plan, I mean?"

She shook her head. "I don't know. I guess I'll have to disappoint him. I mean, I'm not the most outgoing person when it comes to dating, and I don't want to mislead any guys about where it's all headed." She forced a smile. "Know any eligible bachelors I could snare?"

"Me," he heard himself saying. "You could marry me."

Chapter Four

As he watched the color drain from Angelica's face, Troy's chest tightened and he wished he could take back his words. What had he just said? What had he been thinking?

Cynical doubts kicked at the crazy adrenaline rush coursing through his body. Why would he want to propose to Angelica again when she'd dumped him without explanation before? He'd already done what he could to help her and her son. He'd given her a job and provided a place to live, but this was way beyond the call of duty.

He opened his mouth to say so, but she held up a hand.

"Look, it's amazingly kind of you to offer that, especially after…after everything. You've already done so much for us. But I could never expect anything like that. And I couldn't marry someone without…"

He crossed his arms over his chest. "Without loving him?"

"I was going to say…" She lowered her head and let out a sigh. "Never mind."

Suddenly warm, he stood, grabbed a crutch and limped

across the room. He flicked on the air-conditioning and fiddled with the thermostat on the wall.

She'd brought up all the very same objections he'd had himself. She'd given him a way to back out.

So why did he feel so let down?

She scrambled to her feet, watching him as if he were a wild animal she had to protect herself from. All comfort, all closeness between them was gone. "Um, I should go." Her hand on the screen door handle, she stilled. "Uh-oh."

"What's wrong?" He came up behind her and looked over her shoulder out the door as the scent of her hair tickled his nose.

In the outdoor floodlight he saw Xavier was running toward the house, his face furrowed. Teary hiccups became more audible as he got closer. Behind him, Lou Ann followed at a dangerously fast pace, huffing and puffing and calling the boy.

Angelica opened the screen door just as Xavier got to the top of the porch steps. She knelt, and Xavier ran into her arms, causing her to reel backward.

Troy balanced on his crutch and reached out to steady the pair. "Whoa there, partner, slow down!"

"Is it true?" Xavier demanded. "What Miss Lou Ann said?"

At that moment the lady in question arrived at the top of the front porch steps. "Xavier!" She paused for breath. "You come…when I call you. I'm sorry," she added, turning to Angelica. "I said something I shouldn't have. It upset him."

"She said it wasn't going to work out for that man to be my daddy, and I might not get a daddy!"

"Come on in, baby." Angelica scooped her son into her arms and struggled to her feet, shrugging off Troy's attempt to help her. She carried Xavier inside. "Is it okay if we talk a minute in here?"

"Sure."

And then he watched her focus entirely on her son. She sat down on the couch and pulled the boy, all angular arms and long legs, in her lap. "So tell me more about those tears, mister."

"I want a daddy!" he sulked. "I thought you were gonna get me one."

She rubbed his hairless head. "I know how much you want a dad. You want to be like other kids."

"I want somebody to play T-ball with me and take me fishing." Behind the words, Troy heard a poignant yearning for all Xavier wanted and might not get, all he'd missed during the long months of treatment.

"I know," Angelica said, rocking a little. "I know, honey."

"So why did you send that man away?"

She shot a glance at Troy. "He wasn't feeling well."

"So he might come back when he's better?"

Slowly, Angelica shook her head. "No, honey. Turns out he's not right for us."

Tears welled in the boy's eyes again, but she pulled his head against her chest. "Shh. I know it's hard, but we have to let God do His work. He takes care of us, remember?"

"Sometimes He does a bad job!"

Angelica chuckled, a low vibration that brushed along Troy's nerve endings. "He never does a bad job, sweetie. Sometimes you and I can't understand His ways, but He's always taking care of us. We can relax because of that."

Her voice sounded totally confident, totally sure, and Troy wished for some of that certainty for himself.

She was such a good mother. She knew exactly how to reach her son, even when he was upset. She could listen, handle his bratty moments and get him to laugh. She was meant to mother this boy, and most of the resentment Troy felt about her pregnancy fell away. Whatever had happened, whatever mistakes she'd made, she'd paid for them. And as she said, God was always taking care of things. He'd given one sick young boy the perfect mother.

Who, when she met his eyes over the child's head and gave him a little smile, looked like the perfect wife, as well.

A week later, Angelica was chopping vegetables for stew and marveling at how quickly they'd settled into a routine. Lou Ann took an online class every Tuesday and Thursday, so those days, Angelica started dinner for all of them while Xavier rested.

As she chopped the last carrot, though, Xavier burst into the kitchen. "Can I go outside and see Mr. Troy and the dogs?"

Thrilled to see this sign of improved energy, she nonetheless narrowed her eyes at him. "What are you doing off the couch? You're supposed to rest from two to four every afternoon. Doctor's orders."

"I don't want to rest anymore. Besides, it's almost four."

"Is it really?" She looked at the clock. "Three-thirty isn't four, buster." But it was close. Where had the time gone? Troy had been wonderful about letting her set up a flexible schedule around Xavier, but she needed to get back out to the kennels at four. She bit the inside of her cheek.

"I want to go outside." Xavier's lower lip pushed out.

"That's not going to work, honey. After you rest, you need to stay in here with Miss Lou Ann so I can work."

"But I wanna go outside!" Xavier yelled.

Angelica dried her hands on a dishcloth and shot up a prayer for patience. Then she knelt in front of Xavier. "Inside voice and respect, please."

"Sorry." He didn't sound it, but she stood up anyway. With a sick kid, you had to choose your battles.

"I see someone's feeling better." Troy limped into the kitchen, wearing jeans and a collared shirt. His shoulder muscles flexed as he hopped nimbly over on his crutches.

He looks good! was her first thought, and it made her cheeks heat up. "I didn't know you were here today. Thought you had vet patients in town."

"I come home early on Thursdays. Snagged a ride with our receptionist." He was looking at her steadily, eyebrows raised a little, as if he could read her mind. How embarrassing!

Xavier tugged at his leg. "Can I come outside with you, Mr. Troy? Please?"

"It's okay with me, buddy." Troy reached down to pat Xavier's shoulder. "But what does your mom say? She's the boss."

"I can't let him follow you around and bother you."

"I think you and Xavier were at the doctor's last week, so you wouldn't know that Thursdays are special. I do some other stuff."

"Stuff I can do with you?" Xavier was staring up at Troy, eyes wide and pleading.

Angelica bit back a smile. Her son, the master manipulator. "Honey, we have to respect—"

"Actually," Troy interrupted, "this might be a really good activity for Xavier. If you're willing."

"What is it?" She covered the stew pot and lowered the gas heat.

"Dog training. Takes a lot of patience." He winked at her. "Some kid training, too. Let him come with me, and then you come out, too, in a little while. I may need some help."

"Please, Mom?"

She threw up her hands. "I give up. Go ahead."

She watched out the window as Xavier and Troy walked off together. Troy was getting more and more agile with his crutches, and she suspected he'd be off them soon. His head was inclined to hear what Xavier was saying, and as for her son, he was chattering away so joyously that she was glad she'd let him go with Troy.

She wanted him to be happy, and right now, somehow, that happiness was all tied up in Troy. Troy and the dogs. Pray God it would last.

"They look more like father and son than most father and sons," Lou Ann said, walking into the room with an armload of books and paperwork. "That's good for Troy. He didn't have a great relationship with his own dad. Still doesn't, for that matter."

"I remember, but I never knew why." Angelica reached down to scratch Bull's head. "Go back to your bed, buddy. I'm done cooking, and Daddy says no table scraps for you."

"That doesn't keep him from begging, though." Lou Ann put her laptop and books on the built-in desk in the corner of the kitchen. "Clyde Hinton is a hard man, especially with his boys. His older son fought back, and that's why the two of them can work together now. Troy, though, wasn't having any of it. He shut the door on his dad a long time ago. They hardly ever see each other."

"Interesting." During their engagement, she and Troy

hadn't visited much with his father, and the little time they'd spent at Troy's family home was stiff and uncomfortable.

Settling into a chair at the kitchen table, Lou Ann put her feet up on one of the other chairs and stretched. "Where's Xavier going, anyway? I'm ready to play some *Extreme Flight Simulator* with him. Clear my brain from all that psychology."

"Troy's taking him out to the kennels." Angelica turned to the woman who was rapidly becoming a good friend. "I'm so impressed you're working on your degree online."

"Never had the chance before," Lou Ann said, "and it's a kick. I always did like school, just never had time to really pursue it. And Troy insists on paying for it. Says it's the least he can do since I agreed to come back to work for him."

"Wow, I didn't know that."

"There's a lot of things you don't know about that man," Lou Ann said. "He's not one to toot his own horn."

Angelica tucked that away for consideration. "He's sure being good to Xavier. Though he doesn't know what he's getting into, taking him out to the kennels. He'll have to watch him like a hawk, and he won't get any of his own work done."

"It's Thursday, isn't it?" Lou Ann glanced up at the calendar on the wall. "Thursdays, he has the rascals over. Maybe he's going to get Xavier involved with them."

"The rascals, huh?" Just what Xavier needed. "Who are they?"

One side of Lou Ann's mouth quirked up. "They're some kids I wouldn't work with to save my life, but somehow Troy has them helping at the kennel, training dogs and cleaning cages. He's a rescuer, always has been."

"Dangerous kids?" Angelica paused in the act of handing Lou Ann a cup of coffee.

"No, not dangerous. Just full of beans. Relax!" Lou Ann reached for the coffee, took a sip and put it down on the table. "Thanks, hon. There are some real poor folks in this county. Kids who live on hardscrabble farms, hill people just up from down South, migrants who've set up their trailers at the edge of some field."

"Sounds like the way I grew up," Angelica said wryly.

"That's right." Lou Ann looked thoughtful for a minute. "Anyway, when Troy was...well, when he went through a rough spot a while back, Pastor Ricky approached him about setting up a program for those kids. Troy went along, because a lot of them hadn't a notion of the right way to take care of a dog. It's grown, and now he's got ten or twelve coming every week to help out."

"That's amazing, with everything else he does."

"He'd help anyone in the world. What doesn't come so easy to him is taking help himself."

"I'm going to go out." Angelica rinsed the cutting board and stood it in the drainer. "Just as soon as I get those bathrooms clean."

"You go ahead now," Lou Ann said. "I can tell you're a little worried about your boy. I think you'll like what you see."

"Thanks." Impulsively, she gave the older woman a hug.

Five minutes later, Angelica was leaning on the fence outside the kennel, watching Xavier run and play with dogs and boys of all sizes, shapes and colors. He looked so happy that it took Angelica's breath away. She didn't know she was crying until Troy came up beside her and ran a light finger under each eye.

She jerked back, not comfortable with the soft, tender touch.

"You okay?"

She drew in a breath and let it out in a happy sigh. "I'm fine. And I'm so grateful to you for letting Xavier have some normal kid moments."

Troy frowned. "He doesn't get to do stuff like this often?"

She shook her head. "He's been in treatment so much that he hasn't had the chance to play with other boys. Let alone a bunch of dogs."

"It's good for the kids. They need to get their energy out in an accepting environment. And I need someone to play with the dogs. Easy there, Enrique!" he called to a boy who was roughhousing with a small white mutt a little too vigorously.

"Sorry, Señor Troy." The boy in question backed off immediately, then knelt and petted the dog.

"Hey, that's the little dog from the clinic! The owner thought he was going to die!"

Troy nodded, looking satisfied. "He's responding to the medication. He should be able to go back home within a week. I know Darlene will be glad. She calls every couple of days."

She studied Troy's profile. He helped dogs who needed it, owners who couldn't pay, kids who'd grown up without advantages. And of course, he was helping her and Xavier.

"Anyway, thanks for giving my son this opportunity."

When he looked down at her, arms propped on

the fence beside hers, she realized how close together they were.

The thought she'd been squelching for the past week, the topic she'd been dodging the couple of times Troy had brought it up, burst into the front of her mind: he'd asked her to marry him just a week ago. He was a man of his word. She could have this. She could have a home, a farm, a man who liked to help others. Most of all, a father for Xavier.

But she'd struggled so long alone that being here, in this perfect life, felt scary, almost wrong. She didn't deserve it.

The other thing she'd been trying not to think about made its way to the surface. She was tainted, dirty. In his heart, Troy would want someone pure. He'd said it enough times when they were engaged—how important it was to him that she'd never been with anyone, that she'd saved herself for marriage. *"I'm a jealous guy,"* he'd said. *"I want you all for my own."*

She tore her eyes away from him, cleared her throat and focused on Xavier, who was rolling on the grass while a couple of the pit bull puppies, already bigger and steadier than they'd been a week ago, licked his face.

She had to live in the moment and focus on all the benefits this lifestyle was bringing her son. And stay as far as possible away from this man who'd proposed marriage.

Troy was a good person, even a great one, but she wasn't a rescue dog. She needed to be with a man who loved her and could accept her mistakes and her past.

"Mom!" Xavier came over, panting, two high red spots on his cheeks. "This is so much fun. Did you see how I was throwing the Frisbee with the guys?"

When he said "the guys," his tone rang with amazed,

self-conscious pride. He'd never been one of the guys, but it was high time he started. And Troy was helping make that happen. "I missed your Frisbee throwing, buddy," she said, "but I'll watch it the next time, okay?"

When she glanced up at Troy to thank him again, she found him staring down at her with a look in his dark eyes that was impossible to read. Impossible to look away from, too. She caught her breath, licked her lips.

As if from a great distance, she heard Xavier calling her name, felt him tugging at her hand. "Hey, Mom, I had a great idea," he was saying.

She shook her head a little, blinked and turned to look at her son. "What's the idea, honey?"

"Do you think Mr. Troy could be my dad?"

Chapter Five

Xavier's words were still echoing in Troy's mind the next day. He was riding shotgun—man, he hated that, but the doctor hadn't yet cleared him to drive—while his friend Dion Grant drove his van. They were taking a group from their church, including Angelica and Xavier, to weed the garden at the Senior Towers.

"Do you think Mr. Troy could be my dad?"

He listened to the group's chatter as they climbed out of the van and pulled garden tools from the back. *Could* he become Xavier's dad? Angelica's husband?

It seemed as if those questions hovered in the air every time he was around Angelica. She'd never responded to his proposal, and yesterday she'd brushed aside Xavier's words and scolded the child.

But was the thought so repugnant to her? Once, she'd wanted to marry him.

Sure, she'd left him, apparently for someone else, since she immediately became pregnant. Knowing her now, he didn't think she'd cheated on him while they were together; she wouldn't have had that in her.

But if she'd fallen in love with someone else and been

too embarrassed to admit it…maybe when she'd gone to visit her aunt that summer…

The moment he emerged from the driver's seat, a small hand tugged at his. "Dad! Dad!"

"Xavier!" Angelica hurried up behind Xavier and put her hands on his shoulders. "Honey, you can't call Mr. Troy 'Dad.'" Her face was bright red, and she wouldn't meet Troy's eyes.

"It's okay." Troy patted her shoulder.

"No, it's really not." Angelica kept her voice low and nodded sideways toward the row of ladies sitting on the porch of the Senior Towers. "Let's just hope nobody heard. Come on, Zavey Davey," she said, "you have a playdate with your new friend Becka from church."

"A girl?" Xavier groaned.

"Yes, and she's a lot of fun. Her mom said you two were going to hunt for bugs in the park. She has a magnifying glass."

Xavier screwed up his face and looked thoughtful.

"And she's into soccer, so maybe you two can kick around a soccer ball."

"Okay. That's cool."

Troy watched as Angelica led her son toward a one-story house set between the Senior Towers and the town park. Her long hair was caught up in a high ponytail, and she wore old jeans and a T-shirt emblazoned with a Run for Shelter/Stop Domestic Violence logo. When had she gotten time to do a charity run, with all she had on her plate? And how did she manage to put zero time into her appearance and still look absolutely gorgeous?

"Breathe, buddy." His friend Dion gave him a light punch in the arm. "Didn't know she was your baby mama, but half the town will pretty soon."

"What? She's not my baby mama," Troy said automatically, and then met his friend's eyes. "Uh-oh. Who all heard what Xavier just said?"

"Miss Minnie Falcon, for one." Dion nodded toward the front porch of the Senior Towers.

Troy shrugged and lifted his hands, palms up. "Xavier's not my kid, but he wants me to be his dad. Guess he's decided to pretend it's so."

"You could do a lot worse than those two."

"Yeah. Except she dumped me once before, and she doesn't want anything but a professional relationship with me."

"You sure about that, my friend?"

He wasn't sure of anything and he felt too confused to discuss the subject. "Come on, we'd better start weeding or the ladies are going to outshine us."

He'd brought a low lawn chair so he could weed without bending his injured leg. Working the earth, just slightly damp from a recent rain, felt soothing to Troy, and he realized he'd been spending too much time indoors, doing paperwork and staying late at his office in town. The dirt was warm and pungent with an oniony scent. Nearby, he could hear the shouts of kids at the park and the occasional car or truck driving by.

Even after Angelica returned and started weeding across the gardens from him, he didn't sweat it. The jokes and chatter of the group, most of whom knew each other well from years of adult Sunday school class together, made for an easy feeling. He was glad they'd come.

"Hey, beautiful, when did you get back to town?"

The voice, from a passerby, sounded pleasant enough, but he turned to see who was calling a member of the group "beautiful" with the tiniest bit of snarkiness in his tone. It took a minute, but he recognized the guy from a few classes behind him in high school, dressed in a scrub shirt and jeans. Logan Filmore. Brother of a friend of his. Guy must be in some kind of medical field now.

And of course, he was speaking to Angelica.

Troy's eyes flashed to her and read her concern, even distaste.

He pushed to his feet, grabbed a crutch and limped across the garden to stand beside her. "How's it going?"

"Okay." She looked uneasily at Logan, who'd stopped in front of them.

The guy looked at Troy and seemed to read something in his eyes, because he took a step back. He gave Angelica a head-to-toes once-over, then waved and walked on, calling, "Nice to see you" over his shoulder.

Angelica squatted back down and Troy eased himself down beside her.

"Someone you know?"

She yanked a thistle out of the ground. "Sort of."

"Is there anything I can do?"

Another weed hit the heap in the center of the garden. "Stop talking about it?"

He lifted his hands, palms up. "Okay. Just trying to help."

For several minutes they pulled weeds in silence. Troy was totally aware of her, though: the glow of her skin, the fine sheen of sweat on her face, the vigorous, almost angry way she tugged weeds.

Finally she turned her face partway toward him. "I'm sorry. I…I used to know him and I really dislike him. Thanks for coming over."

"Sure." A few more weeds hit the pile. "I like helping you, you know."

"Thanks."

"I like it a lot." He wanted to protect her from people

like the guy who'd just passed by. He wanted to protect her full-time. Of course, he mainly wanted to marry her for Xavier's sake. That was all.

He reached across her to tug on a vine. Their hands brushed.

He was expecting her to jerk away, but she didn't; she just went a little still.

That gave him the hope he needed. "You still haven't answered my question," he said quietly.

"What question was that?"

"About whether you'd marry me."

She laughed a little. "Oh, that."

"Yes, that. Have you thought about it?"

She shut her eyes for a moment. "I've hardly thought of anything else."

"And?"

"And…I don't know."

"Fair enough," he said. "But is there anything I could do to help you decide?"

She gave him a narrow-eyed look and for a moment, he thought she was going to scold him. "Yes," she said finally. "You could tell me why you want to do it."

"That's easy. I want to do it because Xavier wants a dad. And because I like helping you."

Her mouth got a pinched look. If he hadn't known better, he'd have thought she felt hurt. "Those aren't… those aren't the reasons people get married."

"Are they bad reasons, though?"

She shook her head, staring at the ground. "They're not bad, no. They're fine. Kind. Good."

"Then what's standing in the way?"

She shrugged, looked away. There was a fine film of tears over her eyes. "Nothing. I don't know."

"Look," he said, touching her under the chin with

one finger, lifting her face toward his. "Let's do it. Let's surprise Xavier." He didn't know what was making him force the issue.

Maybe something he saw in her eyes. Some part of her wanted to. And maybe it was for Xavier, or mostly so; but he had a funny feeling that she saw him as a man and was drawn to him.

"We'd be doing it for Xavier." She stared at him, her eyes huge.

"Yes, for Xavier. So, are you saying yes?"

"I think I am."

He nodded. "Then…let's seal it with a kiss." He leaned over and ever so gently brushed her lips with his.

It was meant to be just a friendly peck on the lips, but he lingered a couple of seconds, feeling the tingle of awareness he'd felt before but something else, too, something deeper.

She gasped and jerked away. "We'll…have to figure out…what kind of boundaries…" She trailed off, still staring at him. "You know."

She looked so appealing that he wanted to kiss her again, a real kiss. But the defenseless look on her face got to him and he pulled her into his arms, as slow and light and careful as if she were a wounded animal. "We'll figure it out," he whispered into her soft, dark hair.

"Mom! Can I? Can I?"

Angelica turned away from the church group and from Troy, standing just a little too close for comfort, to greet her son. It was late afternoon, and they were all saying their goodbyes in front of the weeded, re-mulched Senior Towers gardens.

Running ahead of Becka and her mom, Xavier looked

so…normal. His striped shirt was mud-stained, his legs pumping sturdily beneath thrift-store gym shorts. Joy flooded her to see how healthy he looked. And what a relief to get out of the sticky, messy, impossibly emotional situation with Troy and back to what grounded her.

"Can you what, honey?" She knelt to catch Xavier as he ran into her arms, relishing the sweaty, little-boy smell of him.

"Can I play soccer with Becka? Her mom is the coach of the team!"

She hugged him close. "We'll see."

"You say that when you mean no!" Xavier pulled away. "Please, Mom?"

Becka and her mom arrived and Angelica stood up. "Thanks so much for watching him," she said.

"Well, I may have done something wrong." Becka's mom wore shorts and a T-shirt, her hair back in a no-nonsense ponytail under a baseball cap. "Becka and I were talking about soccer practice tonight, and when Xavier was interested, I told him he could join the team."

Angelica felt her eyebrows draw together. "Hmm. I'm not sure."

"Mom!"

"We'll have to see." Angelica bit her lip. She wanted him to be able to do it, to do everything a normal, healthy boy could do, but… "Soccer's pretty strenuous, isn't it?"

"At this age? No more so than normal play." Linda Mason gave her trademark grin. "The kids run around a lot, yeah. And I try to teach them some skills. But it's not competitive. It's just for fun."

"Practice is tonight, Mom!"

"Tonight?" Xavier hadn't had his usual afternoon rest. "I don't think so, sweetie. That's just too much."

A light touch warmed her shoulder. Troy. Her heart skittered as she looked back at him.

He raised an eyebrow, squeezed her shoulder once and then reached out to shake Linda's hand. "Hey, Linda. He'd need a sports physical anyway, wouldn't he?"

"Exactly." Linda nodded. "What we could do, if you don't think it's too much, is to have him come over to the park for a half-hour practice session I do with some of the kids, before the official practice. But you're right, Troy, he couldn't actually be on the team until getting a physical."

Angelica flashed Troy a grateful smile. She hadn't known that kids needed physicals for team sports, and it made the perfect delay tactic.

Xavier's face fell, and tears came to his eyes. "I just wanna play!"

"Then you have to get a physical, buddy!" Angelica gave him a one-armed hug. "All the kids have to get physicals. I'm sure Becka did, right?"

"Yeah, and I had to get a shot."

Xavier grimaced. "Yuck."

As the kids started comparing horror stories about doctors and needles, the three adults sat down on the bench outside the Senior Towers. "I'm really sorry," Linda said. "I didn't mean to get him all excited. But he seems like a great kid, and he had so much fun kicking around a ball with Becka. I'm sure he'd be good at soccer."

"We'll see what the doctor says," Troy said.

Angelica stared at him. "Excuse me?"

"Um, I'm going to go check on the kids." Linda

looked from one to the other, frank curiosity in her eyes. "If that half-hour practice is okay, I'll walk them over to the park. Come on over and watch."

"Okay," Angelica said distractedly as Linda herded the kids toward the park. What did Troy mean, acting as if he had some say in Xavier's life? "Look, I'm sure you didn't mean it this way, but it sounded like you thought we'd all go to the doctor together."

"That's what I was thinking." Troy raised his eyebrows and met her eyes. "Is that a problem?"

"I don't want you to think you're the authority on Xavier after knowing him for, what, three weeks?"

"I can tell," Troy said mildly. "But after all, I'm going to be his father."

Angelica stared at him, momentarily speechless. Adrenaline flooded her body, and her breathing quickened.

She'd have to set some boundaries. She was so used to having full say about Xavier and what he did, how he lived—whether he could play soccer, for instance—and now Troy was wanting to get all high-handed.

In most matters, she'd be fine collaborating with Troy. But where Xavier was concerned, not so much.

"Some people say a two-parent family is good for this very reason." Troy sounded maddeningly calm. "A lot of moms are a little more protective. Dads help kids get out there and see the world."

"Look, you have no experience being a parent, and you don't know what Xavier's been through."

"Come on, let's walk. You want to see him play, don't you?"

"Um…yes! Of course!" Angelica stood, feeling a stiffness in her neck that bespoke a headache to come. "But we're not done talking about this."

How had Troy so smoothly taken control? She had to admit, looking up at him as he strode by her side, ushering her around a broken spot in the sidewalk, nodding to people he knew, that something about his confidence felt good. That it attracted her. She had to admit it, but... "Listen, this is making me a little uncomfortable," she said. "I'm used to having control of Xavier, and I'm not sure I'm willing to give that up."

He nodded. "I understand. I feel like I should have some say, but of course, you're his mom."

"And I make the decisions."

He slanted his eyes down at her. "Right. Okay. You make...the final decisions. Right."

She had to laugh. "Boy, that was pretty hard for you to say. Control much, do you?"

"You know me."

She did. She'd known him for a long time. But this new, older version, a little less driven, a little more humble... Wow. Despite all the craziness in her life, a core of excitement and hope was building inside her.

They approached the park together. Large oaks and maples provided shade against the late-afternoon sun, shining bright in a sky spotted with a few puffy white clouds. Kids shouted and ran around the old-fashioned swings and slide. Ragweed and earth scents mingled with the savory smell of someone's grilled burgers.

On the other side of town, a train on its late afternoon run made a forlorn whistle.

A family sprawled on a blanket together: Mom, Dad, a boy about Xavier's age and a toddler girl with curly red hair and an old-fashioned pink romper. The little girl put her arms around the boy and hugged him, and the father and mother exchanged a smile. Angelica's heart caught. That was what she'd always longed for: a loving man who could share in the raising of the children. A little sister for Xavier.

But that wasn't in the cards for her. What Troy was proposing was purely a marriage of convenience. She had to remember the limits, the reason he'd proposed at all: he wanted to help her, and especially to help Xavier. It wasn't romantic, it wasn't love. Nothing of the kind. Troy was a rescuer, and she and Xavier just so happened to be in need of some rescuing.

They walked over to the area where Linda was leading Xavier, Becka and three other kids through some soccer drills. "He seems to be doing okay," Troy said. "What do you think?"

Tugging her thoughts away from what couldn't be changed, she studied her son, noticing the high spots of color in his cheeks. "He's getting tired. But I'll let him stay for the half hour. I'll make sure he gets some extra rest tomorrow."

They sat down on the bleachers by the soccer field. Troy took her hand and squeezed it, and warmth and impossible hope flooded through her.

"We should talk about those other boundaries," Troy said.

"What…oh." When she saw the meaningful look in his eyes she knew exactly what he was talking about. The physical stuff.

"I'm attracted to you. You can probably tell."

Angelica looked down. She was attracted to him, too, or she thought she was. What else would her breathless, excited feeling be about? But she was too afraid to say so. Too afraid to tell him about all her issues. She pulled her hand away and pressed her lips together to keep herself from blurting out this shameful part of her past.

After a minute, he let out a sigh. "We don't have to

hold hands or kiss or anything like that. I know you're doing this for Xavier, not for love. I want the same thing. I want to take care of you and Xavier, but I won't put pressure on you."

"Right." Her heart felt as if it were shrinking in her chest.

"Now, what about our…personal lives?" He looked at her sideways, raising an eyebrow.

Did he have any idea how handsome he was? "What?"

"I mean your…social life."

What was he talking about?

"Other men, Angelica."

"Other…ooooh." She shook her head. "It's not an issue. I don't date." In fact, she'd never really been in love with anyone but Troy.

"You sure?" He looked skeptical.

"I'm sure!" She looked away. This was the best someone like her could hope for.

Other families were arriving for the soccer game. Mothers in pretty clothes with designer handbags, kids with proper soccer garb. In her garden-stained jeans and T-shirt, carrying her discount-store purse, Angelica wondered if she could ever fit in. If the other families would look askance at Xavier for his murky background, his lack of a father, his mismatched, thrift-shop clothes.

Being with Troy was a chance to be a real part of the community. She wouldn't impose on him to buy her fancy things, but she'd happily accept decent clothing and soccer duds for Xavier. Would happily accept Troy's good name in the town, too, paving the way for her son to be accepted and have friends.

Troy was giving her a lot, and he was even saying he wouldn't expect the physical side of marriage in return.

She should be grateful instead of wanting more.

Chapter Six

Two days later, on a rainy Monday, Angelica was cleaning out kennels when the door burst open and two women stalked in, slamming it behind them.

"Where is he?" one of them asked loudly over the dogs' barking.

She started to put down her shovel and then paused, wondering if she should keep it for self-defense. "Where's who?"

"The boy. Xavier."

Angelica's fingers tightened on the handle of the shovel. "Why do you want to see Xavier?"

As the dogs' barking subsided, one of the women stepped forward into the light, and Angelica recognized her. "Daisy! I haven't seen you in—"

Troy's sister, Daisy, held out one hand like a stop sign. "Don't try to be nice."

Angelica studied the woman she'd once called a friend. Just a couple of years older than Angelica, she wore purple harem pants and a gold shirt. Her hair flowed down her shoulders in red curls, and rings glittered on every finger. Short, adorably chubby and always full of life, she'd been Angelica's main ally in

Troy's family back when she and Troy were engaged. Angelica had hoped they'd be friends again one day.

But Daisy pointed a finger at Angelica. "I want to see my nephew, and I want to see him now."

"Your nephew? Wait a minute. What's going on? What's got you mad?"

"What's got me mad is that I have a nephew who's six years old and I've never even met him. I may not ever be going to have children of my own, but I've always wanted to be an aunt. And now I hear I've been one for years and the boy's been kept from me!"

"Oh, Daisy." Things were starting to fall into place. "Xavier isn't your nephew."

The other woman, whom Angelica didn't recognize, stepped forward—tall and thin, with streaked hair and Asian features. "We heard it on good faith from Miss Minnie Falcon."

Of course. The day of weeding at the Senior Towers. News traveled fast. Angelica shook her head. "Come on, you guys. Sit down. Miss Minnie's got it wrong, but I can explain."

"You've got some explaining to do, all right." Daisy made her way over to Troy's office area and pulled out the desk chair, clearly at home here. "I was already mad at you for what you did to Troy, but this beats all. And I'm sorry, but you were engaged to Troy, and then you left, and now you have a kid. How can he not be my nephew?"

Angelica perched on a crate and gestured to the other woman to do the same.

The woman held out a hand to Angelica. "I'm Susan, Daisy's best friend," she said, "and I'm here to keep her from becoming violent."

"It's nothing to joke about!" Daisy glared at her friend.

Angelica leaned forward. "Daisy, I can tell you for sure that Troy isn't Xavier's father." She explained Xavier's desire for a father and how he'd wishfully called Troy Dad.

"But word was you and Troy were all over each other," Daisy said skeptically.

"All over each other." Angelica rubbed her chin. She was tempted to tell the ladies what was really going on, except she hated to do that without Troy. They hadn't had the chance to discuss what they'd tell the world about their so-called engagement; Xavier didn't even know, because once Xavier knew, everyone in town would know.

She needed time to prepare, but there wasn't any. "Listen," she said, "I'm gonna go get Troy."

"Don't you try to hide behind him. He's a sucker where you're concerned."

"Daisy," the other woman said in a low voice. "We shouldn't judge. Especially considering we came straight from Bible group."

"Even Jesus got righteously angry." Daisy sulked, but then she nodded at her friend. "You're right. I'm not giving you much of a chance, Angelica, am I? But the truth is, I always really liked you, and when you dumped Troy, you dumped me, too. And now to hear that you've actually had a baby… That pretty much beats all."

"Let me get Troy."

"No, I'll text him."

Before Angelica could stop her, Daisy was on her phone, and a couple of minutes of awkward small talk later, Troy walked in. "What's going on?"

Angelica's mind raced through the possible outcomes of this confrontation. They weren't great. If they didn't reveal their marriage of convenience now, it would make Daisy mad, and as Daisy went, so went the family. On the other hand, if they did explain that it wasn't a real marriage, that would get out, too. And that was exactly what she didn't want Xavier to find out.

Without thinking it through, she walked over to Troy and put an arm around him. "Honey," she said. "Can we spill the beans a tiny bit early and tell Daisy and Susan our news?"

When Angelica put her arm around him, Troy almost fell off his crutches. She was so resistant to getting physically close that her act of affection stunned him. It took another moment for him to realize what she'd said.

Really? She wanted to tell his sister, who knew everyone in town and loved to talk, about their pseudo-engagement?

Troy blinked in the dark kennel. Automatically, he hobbled over—his leg was bad today—toward one of the barking dogs in the front, a fellow named Crater for the ugly scar in the middle of his back, and opened the gate of his kennel. Crater leaped with joy and Troy knelt awkwardly to rub and pet him.

Then he looked back at Angelica.

She cocked her head to one side and raised her eyebrows. She must have had a reason for what she'd done; she wasn't one to playact for no reason. And if he was going to marry her, maybe even to make it a good marriage, he needed to show her his trust. "Are you sure about this?"

"I think we should tell them." She was communicating with her eyes, willing him to say something, and he only hoped he'd get it right.

"Okay," he said, pushing himself to his feet and limping over to drape an arm around Angelica's shoulders. "Guys…Angelica and I have decided to get married."

There were no happy hugs, no shouts of joy. Daisy's lips pressed together. "Are you sure that's a good idea?"

"Of course," he said. "We've…settled our differences." He tightened his arm around Angelica for emphasis and noticed that she was shaking. "Hey, it's okay. It's Daisy. She'll be happy for us!" He glared at his sister. "Won't you?"

"Are you kidding?" Daisy was nothing if not blunt. "I can't be happy to watch you setting yourself up for another fall."

He felt Angelica cringe.

"Daisy!" Susan put a hand on her hip. "Be nice."

Troy rubbed Angelica's shoulder a little, still feeling her tension. "Look, the past is water under the bridge. We've started over, and we'd appreciate it if you would be supportive." He frowned at Daisy. "For all of us, especially Xavier."

He watched as his opinionated sister struggled with herself. Finally she nodded. "All right," she said. "I'll do my best."

Angelica chimed in. "You said you'd always wanted to be an aunt. Well, now you'll be one. Xavier will be thrilled to have a bigger family. We've been pretty much…" She cleared her throat. "Pretty much on our own, since my aunt passed away."

For the millionth time, he wondered what had happened to make her leave him and leave town. And what had happened to Xavier's father.

Apparently he wasn't the only one. "One thing I've

got to know," Daisy said. "Who's Xavier's father if it's not Troy?"

The question hung in the air. It was what Troy had wanted to ask but hadn't had the guts to. Trust Daisy to get the difficult topics out into the open.

Angelica didn't speak. She was staring at the ground as if the concrete floor held the answer to Daisy's question.

"Well?" Daisy prompted. "If we're all starting fresh, what better basis than honesty?"

Angelica looked up, shot a glance at Troy and then lifted her chin and met Daisy's eyes. "I'm not at liberty to share that information," she said. "It's Xavier's story, and when he's old enough, he'll decide who he wants to share it with. Until then, it's private."

"Does he even know?" Daisy blurted.

"No!" Angelica stood, crossed her arms and paced back and forth. "And I'd appreciate all of you avoiding the topic with him. He's not old enough to understand, and I don't want him to start questioning. Not yet."

Something ugly twisted in Troy's chest. He wanted to know, if only so he could watch out for the guy, keep him away from her in the future, know his enemy. To have that unknown rival out there made the hairs on the back of his neck stand up.

"I guess that makes sense," Daisy said doubtfully.

"Thank you for respecting my son's right to privacy."

As he accepted the forced hugs of his sister and pretended to be an excited, normal fiancé to Angelica, Troy had to wonder whether they were doing the right thing.

"I don't know, man." Troy's friend Dion, the police chief of Rescue River, sat across from him at the table of the Chatterbox Café later that afternoon. They were drinking coffee and Troy had confided the truth about the marriage of convenience, knowing Dion could keep a secret. "I just don't know. You say you're doing it for Xavier, but Father God has His plans for that boy. What if He takes him young, him being so sick with leukemia? You going to divorce Angelica then?"

"No!" Troy's coffee cup clattered into the saucer, liquid sloshing over the sides. "I wouldn't leave her, not in her time of need, not ever."

"Think she'll stay with you?"

Troy drew in a breath and let it out in a sigh. "I hope so, but I can't know for sure. She left me before."

"And she won't tell you who the daddy is?"

Troy shook his head. "Says it's between her and Xavier, and she doesn't want the whole town to know before he does. Says it's his story to tell."

Dion shook his head. "That's a nice theory. But a man and his wife shouldn't have secrets." He rubbed a hand over his nearly shaved head. "Secrets destroy a marriage. I'm living proof of that."

Troy nodded. Dion didn't talk much about his marriage, but Troy knew there had been rough patches. Then they'd straightened things out, and then Dion's wife had passed away. Dion had turned to God and he had a deeper faith than anyone else Troy knew, which was why he'd come to his friend with his own issue. "Do I try to force it out of her, though?" he asked. "Is it even my right to know?"

"All kinds of reasons to know about paternity," Dion pointed out. He paused while the waitress, a little too interested in their conversation, poured them some more coffee. "Thanks, Felicity," he said to her. "We won't be needing anything else."

After she left, Troy chuckled. "She's curious what

we're talking about, and she's even more curious what you're doing Friday night."

Dion shook his head. "Got a date with the baseball game on TV, just like usual. Anyway, what if something happened to Angelica? You'd need to know Xavier's story. For his health, if nothing else, it's important to know who his daddy is."

"I guess."

"Something else. Everybody in town gonna think you're the daddy. Some already do. You okay with that?"

"What people say doesn't matter."

Dion looked out the window, a little smile on his face. "Maybe not," he said finally. "But you won't look like the good guy anymore. People might think you've been neglecting your duties."

"What the gossips say doesn't matter. Period."

"Okay." Dion studied him. "I believe you. Still, you gotta know."

"You've convinced me of that."

"Talk to her, man. But pray first. Because it's not easy to be calm about the guy who got your girl pregnant, but in this situation, calm is what you'll have to be."

Troy nodded thoughtfully. How was he going to bring this up? One thing Dion was sure right about—he needed every bit of help the good Lord could offer him. Only thing was, he hated asking for help of any kind. Even from God.

Chapter Seven

Angelica was in the kitchen washing breakfast dishes when she heard the screeching of brakes out on the road.

"Zavey?"

No answer.

She grabbed a dish towel on her way out the door, drying her hands as she climbed the slight rise to where she could see the road.

Her heart seemed to stop. Xavier was on his knees beside the road, screaming.

She practically flew over the ground until she reached him and saw the situation.

In front of Xavier, a couple of feet from the edge of the road, Bull lay in the gravel, his sturdy body twisted at an odd angle. A car was pulled halfway into the ditch across the road, and in front of it, a middle-aged woman pressed her hand to her mouth.

Heart pounding, Angelica knelt by her son, patting his arms and legs, examining him. "Are you okay?"

Xavier gulped and nodded and pointed toward Bull. "I'm… It's my fault… I let him off his lead. I wanted him to play fetch." His voice rose to a wail. "I think he's dead."

"I'm sorry, I'm so sorry!" The driver came over and sank to her knees beside them, her voice shaking, tears streaking her face. "I didn't see the dog, he came running out so fast..."

And suddenly Troy was there, kneeling awkwardly beside Bull.

"Oh, honey." Angelica scooped Xavier up into her arms, reached out a hand to pat the stranger's shoulder and leaned toward Troy and Bull, her heart aching at the sight of the still, twisted dog. "Is...is he alive?"

Busy examining Bull, Troy didn't answer, so she set Xavier down and instructed him to stay out of Troy's way. She took information from the distraught driver and walked her back to her vehicle, promising to call and let her know how the dog was, making sure the woman was calm enough to drive and able to back her car out of the ditch.

And then she knelt beside Troy and Xavier, putting her arm around her son.

"I'm sorry I let him off his lead! It's my fault!" Xavier buried his face in her shoulder, weeping.

"Shh. It was an accident. You didn't know." She bit her lip and touched Troy's arm. "Is he breathing?"

Troy took one quick glance toward them and then went back to examining the dog. "Yes, but he's pretty badly injured. I'd like to do surgery right away. Here. No time to get to town." He scanned the area. "Can you grab me a big board out of the shed? There's a stack beside the door."

"Of course. Xavier, stay here." She ran to the shed and came back with a piece of plywood.

"Give me your hoodie," Troy was saying to Xavier. "I'm going to wrap Bull up in it. T-shirt, too, buddy."

Xavier shucked his hoodie and started pulling off his T-shirt, shivering in the chilly morning air.

Her son was so vulnerable to colds. "But, Troy, he shouldn't—"

"I can do it, Mom!" Xavier's trembly voice firmed up and he sniffed loudly and wiped his face on the T-shirt before handing it over to Troy.

"We need to keep Bull warm," Troy explained in a calm voice, slipping out of his own much larger T-shirt and kneeling to cover the old bulldog. "And," he said, lowering his voice so only Angelica could hear, "Xavier needs to help."

Gratitude spread through Angelica's chest. "Thank you." She knelt and helped him ease the dog onto the wide wooden plank she'd found.

Bull yelped once and his old eyes opened, then closed again. His breathing came in hard bursts.

Together, Angelica and Troy lifted the makeshift stretcher. Once, Troy lurched hard to one side, and it took both Xavier and Angelica to steady Bull. Angelica's heart twisted when she saw that a smear of blood had gotten on Xavier's hand. With his medical history, he was oversensitive to blood.

But he just wiped his hand on his jeans. "Where are your crutches, Mr. Troy?"

"Dumped 'em. Come on."

Worry pinged Angelica's heart. Troy had been to the doctor just yesterday and had gotten another full cast and a warning that he was putting too much weight on his leg.

"Can you fix him?" Xavier asked as they walked toward the kennel building.

Troy glanced down at Xavier. "They say I'm good,"

he tried to joke, but his voice cracked. He was limping badly now.

Angelica gulped in a breath. "Who can I call to help?"

"Buck's my only trained surgical assistant, but I'm not having him on the property. I'll manage."

"I'll help as best I can." But how would she do that? she wondered; Lou Ann wasn't here and Xavier needed her. He couldn't watch the surgery.

They got Bull to the kennel and onto the small examining table Troy had for emergencies.

"You've gotta fix him, Mr. Troy! I love him!"

"I know, son." Troy turned to Xavier. "Watch him, and if he starts to move, hold him while I wash up and prep. Angelica, you help him."

"Okay. But I don't think Xavier should stick around."

By the time Troy had assembled his instruments and gotten back to the dog, he had to lean hard on the operating table, and Angelica saw his face twist with pain.

How would he stand, possibly for several hours, and do delicate surgery without help?

Angelica hurried Xavier outside and pulled out her phone. Buck had given her his number when they were going to go out, and hopefully… Good, she'd never deleted it. She hit the call button.

"Hey, Angie," he said, sounding sleepy.

"I've got an emergency," she said, not bothering to greet him. "Listen, are you sober?"

"Yeah. Just woke up."

"Can you come out to the farm and help Troy with a surgery? Bull is hurt."

"Be right there."

She went back in and helped Troy hold Bull still and

administer something with a needle. As he ran careful hands over the dog's leg, his face was set, jaw clenched.

"Is he gonna be okay, Mr. Troy?" Xavier asked from the doorway.

Angelica and Troy met each other's eyes over the table.

"I don't know," Troy said, his voice husky. "I'm going to do my very best. You've been a big help."

The dog's laceration looked bad, but as Troy continued to examine it, his face relaxed a little. "I don't think any internal organs are affected, though we can't be sure about that. It's the leg I'm worried about. I'll try to pin it, but I'm not sure it'll work."

"You can fix him. Right?" Xavier's voice was hopeful.

Troy turned to her son. "It's hard to tell," he said. "He's an older guy, and I had to give him strong medicine to make him sleep. That's hard on him. And his leg might be the more serious injury. We just don't know, buddy."

The anesthetic had set in and Troy was just starting to clean the wound when a car sounded. "Can you see who that is?" Troy said without looking up.

She went out, opened the door and let Buck in. "He's just getting started," she said. "Let me walk back with you. He doesn't know you're here."

Buck, already dressed in scrubs, followed her in.

"Troy, I have Buck here to help you."

Troy's shoulders stiffened. "How'd you manage that?"

"I have his number from before."

No answer.

"Stone-cold sober, man, and ready to help." Buck pulled on some gloves. He glanced up at Troy's face.

"Whoa, chill. I'm here by invitation. And truth is, you look like you could use the help. Sure you didn't get hit, too?"

Troy's glance at Angelica was as cold as ice.

She swallowed hard. "I'm going to tend to Xavier. He needs to get inside, get cleaned up and rest."

"Fine." He turned away.

Letting her know things were anything but fine.

The surgery took longer than Troy expected, and operating on his own pet threw professional objectivity right out the window. Armstrong's help was crucial, but even with it, the outcome was touch and go.

Discouraged, his leg on fire with the pain of standing without support for several hours, Troy cleaned up while Buck finished bandaging Bull. Troy watched the younger man easily manage the heavy dog in one arm while he opened the crate door with the other, and the anger he'd shoved aside during the delicate surgery rushed back in.

Since when was Angelica in touch with Buck? How often did they talk, get together? Why hadn't she mentioned the friendship if, in fact, it was innocent?

He could barely manage to thank Buck, and the other man's cheerful "Anytime, my man" rang as guilty in Troy's ears. When they walked out together, Buck held the door for him and then checked his phone and jogged off toward his Jeep and swung in. Leaving Troy to hobble toward the house on both crutches, wanting nothing more than some pain medication and a place to put his leg up.

Angelica greeted him at the door. "How is he?"

Just looking at her made his stomach roil. "The dog or your boyfriend?"

She paled. "What?"

He clenched his jaw. "Bull is resting peacefully, but it'll be a few days before we know how well he does. He did come out of the anesthesia, so he's at least survived that."

"Oh, that's wonderful." She backed away from the door to let him by. "But, Troy, what did you mean by that other crack?"

He spun, faced her down. "Why did you keep Armstrong's phone number? How long have you had something going on with him?"

Her forehead wrinkled. "I don't have anything going on with anybody."

To Troy's ears, her denial sounded forced. He squeezed his eyes shut and turned away from her. "I'm beat. I'm going to get some rest."

"I'll take care of the dogs," she said, her voice hesitant. "But I don't want to have this stand between us. I had Buck's phone number because I never deleted it from before. Not because I'm seeing him."

"Yeah, right." Troy had heard so many denials all his life. He remembered his mother's lies to his father, remembered the first time he'd seen her driving by with another man and realized that she wasn't telling the truth about her whereabouts.

Angelica herself had left him to sleep with another man.

It crushed him that Angelica was seeing Buck. He'd half expected something like this to happen, but not so soon. He'd never thought she would cheat on him even before the wedding.

In fact, he'd even thought she had feelings for him. He felt his shoulders slump, as if the bones that held up his body had turned to jelly. Women were treacherous and his own meter of awareness was obviously broken.

Fool that he was.

"Listen," she said now, stepping in front of him as he tried to leave the room. A high flush had risen to her cheeks, and her eyes sparked fire. "I don't appreciate what you're accusing me of. I have no feelings for Buck. I barely know the man."

He leaned against the wall as exhaustion set in. "You were all set to date him. The only obstacle was his drinking. Well, he's sober today, so go for him."

"I. Don't. Want. Him. I never did. And anyway, I'm getting married to you."

"Yeah, well, we both know how real that marriage is," he said bitterly. "It's a sham, for your convenience and Xavier's. You said you never dated, but obviously that wasn't true."

"You're not listening."

"I don't listen to lies."

She shook her head, staring at him, her brown eyes gone almost black. "You're insulting my integrity and I don't appreciate that. I'm committed to you until we decide different. Which it looks like you're doing right now."

"It's not me who made the decision to seek comfort elsewhere." He rubbed the back of his neck. "Tell me, when you act all scared about being touched, is that fake? Or are you just repulsed by me?"

"Is it… Oh man." Her hands went to her hips. "You are making me so mad, Troy Hinton. Just because your parents had their problems—and yeah, I know about that, I heard it from your sister—it doesn't mean you get free rein to accuse me of whatever other women have done to you."

"I'm not…" He paused. Maybe he was. He didn't know. "Look, I'm too tired to think. Can we just put this whole conversation on hold for now?"

"What, so you can build up even more of a case against me? No way." She was small but she was determined and she obviously wasn't budging. "I'm not letting you do this, Troy. I'm not letting you fall in hate with me."

"Why not? Wouldn't it be easier for you?"

She heaved out a sigh and looked up at the ceiling. "No, it wouldn't be easier and it wouldn't be right. Stop judging me!"

"I wasn't—"

"Yes, you were," she pressed on, stepping in closer. "To think I'm dating Buck in all my spare time—which if you haven't noticed, is nonexistent—is totally insulting. As well as ridiculous. So can it and apologize before I whack you one."

That unexpected image made him smile. "You're scaring me, Angelica."

"Mom will do it, too. What do you mean, Mom's dating Buck ? And how's Bull?"

They both froze. In the doorway stood Xavier, in sweats and a T-shirt, his hair sticking up in all directions. He swayed a little and grabbed on to the door frame.

Angelica knelt before him, steadying him with a hand on his shoulder. "Honey! I didn't know you were up from your rest."

"I heard you guys fighting. Is Bull okay?" He looked plaintively up at Troy.

Hard as it was to kneel on one leg with his casted leg stuck awkwardly out beside him, he got himself down to Xavier's level. "Bull is sleeping. The drugs we gave him during the surgery made him tired. But he's looking pretty good for an old guy."

Xavier wasn't to be placated with that. "Is he gonna die?"

Troy's heart clenched in his chest. This was a kid too familiar with death. "I can't promise you that he won't, because he's an old dog. The accident was hard on him, and surgery is, too. But I did my best, and we're going to take good care of him. Okay?"

"Can I see him?"

Troy glanced at Angelica. "How about we bring him inside in a couple of hours, once he's gotten some rest? Okay?"

Angelica and Xavier nodded, both looking serious, and Troy's chest clenched painfully. He cared for both of them way too much. He wanted to protect them, wanted to answer Xavier's questions, wanted to help him heal.

Wanted to trust Angelica.

Now that he'd come down from his angry high, now that he was looking at the sunshine on her black hair as she leaned forward to hug her son, he thought he must have been crazy to accuse her.

But at the same time, there was that nagging doubt.

"You better get some rest, Troy." Angelica's tone was guarded. "And we'll do the same, right, Zavey? We'll have a quiet day. Because tomorrow, we get to go meet your teacher and see your classroom. Just a couple of weeks until school starts."

Troy nudged Xavier with his crutch. "That's a big deal, buddy. You're going to have a blast."

Concern darkened Angelica's eyes and she was biting her lip. He knew she wanted Xavier to go to school, wanted him to have as normal a life as possible for as long as possible.

He headed toward the stairs but turned back to look at Angelica. She was ushering Xavier toward the door, but he was dawdling over a handheld video game. Angelica stopped, looking half patient and half exasperated, and then she squeezed her eyes shut. He saw her lips moving.

He felt like an utter cad. She was dealing with the worst thing a mother could face, the possible death of her child, and doing it beautifully, focusing on Xavier and his needs. Given his health issues, educating him at home would have been easier, but Xavier was a social kid and needed friends, so she'd called umpteen social workers and school administrators and the school nurse to figure out a way he could attend as much as possible and make up his work when he had to be out. She was super stressed out, and how had he supported her?

By calling her out for cheating, when she'd just been trying to help him. At least he thought so.

He scrubbed a hand over his face and headed up the stairs. Reopening their discussion would likely just result in more misunderstanding. He had to get a little rest.

And then he'd get up and be a better man. With God's help.

Chapter Eight

As soon as the school secretary buzzed them in, Angelica marched into Xavier's new elementary school—her own alma mater—holding Xavier by one hand.

Immediately memories assailed her, brought on by the smell of strong cleaning chemicals and the sight of cheerful, bright alphabet letters hanging from the ceiling. She could almost feel the long patchwork skirt brushing her first-grade legs and taste the peanut-butter-and-sprouts sandwiches that had marked her as just a little different from the other kids.

Behind her, Gramps was breathing hard, and she paused to hold the office door open for him. Gramps had driven them there because he knew how important this was. They all wanted to see Xavier have a real childhood, and a big part of that was a regular school.

The other reason Gramps had driven her was that Troy had taken the truck to drive himself and Bull into town today for a consultation with another vet. He wasn't supposed to drive with his cast, but he'd insisted that they keep this appointment for Xavier, that he could manage driving with his left foot.

She knew the real reason he didn't want her to drive

him: he was still a little mad at her. Well, fine. She was mad at him, too. Things hadn't been the same since he had accused her of dating Buck on the sly, an idea that would be laughable except he so obviously took it seriously.

It made her feel hopeless about their relationship. If he was that quick to suspect her morals when she'd called Buck in to help him, how would he react to finding out about her assault?

And underneath her anger, a dark thread of shame twisted through her gut. She *had* gone out drinking. She'd even flirted. If she hadn't, if she'd stayed safely at home by herself, she wouldn't have been assaulted.

But she couldn't think about that now; she had to gear up to fight yet another battle for Xavier. Had to get the right teacher and the best classroom situation for him. "Hello, I'm here to see Dr. Kapp," she said to the plump, middle-aged secretary who was working the desk in the front office.

"Okay, and this must be Xavier," the woman said, smiling down at him. "Welcome to your new school! Dr. Kapp will be right out."

Xavier's grin was so wide it made his eyes crinkle and his cheeks go round as red apples.

Meanwhile, Angelica took deep breaths, trying not to be nervous. Dr. Kapp had always been strict, and she must be ancient now, probably even more set in her ways. How would she respond to Angelica, who'd been notorious in the town for having parents who bummed around in their ancient Volkswagen minivan, spent too much time in bars and sold weed?

While Gramps and Xavier looked at a low showcase of children's art, Angelica tried to forget about Troy and prepare for the battle ahead.

Please, Lord, help me remember. I'm not that mixed-up little hippie girl anymore. I'm Your child and You're here with me.

"Well, Angelica Camden! It's been a long time." Dr. Kapp's tone was dry. "So you have a son now."

Was that accusation in her voice? Angelica couldn't be sure, but she felt it. "Hello," she said, extending her hand to the woman whose close-cropped hair and dark slacks and jacket still made her look like an army general. *God's child. God's child.* "It *has* been a long time."

"I know you're here to talk about your son, but I think we have all the necessary information." Dr. Kapp's eyebrows went up, suggesting Angelica was wasting her time. "Was there something else before you meet Xavier's teacher and see the classroom?"

Angelica glanced back at Gramps for support, but he'd sat down heavily in one of the chairs in the waiting section of the office. Xavier had come over to press against her leg in an uncharacteristic display of neediness. So he was scared, too.

Angelica swallowed. "I'd like to talk to you about Xavier's placement in first grade." She'd rehearsed these words, but her voice still wobbled like the little girl she'd been. She drew in a deep breath. "I understand one of the first-grade teachers is a man, and I'd like for him to be in that class."

Dr. Kapp nodded. "A lot of parents want to choose their child's teacher, but we don't do things that way. I've placed Xavier in Ms. Hayashi's classroom. I think you'll like her."

"Go see if Gramps wants to play tic-tac-toe," Angelica said to Xavier, who was staring up at Dr. Kapp with a sort of awe.

Once he'd gotten out of earshot, she spoke quickly.

"I'm a single mother, and that's why I'd like for him to have a male influence."

Dr. Kapp nodded. "That's understandable, but from what you said on the phone, Xavier may have some special needs. That's why we've placed him in Ms. Hayashi's class. She's dual-certified in special education, and I think she's the best choice for Xavier."

So Dr. Kapp wasn't just being autocratic. Angelica bit her lip. "Yes, the doctors said his chemo might have caused some cognitive delays, so a teacher who gets that makes a difference, for sure. I just…don't have many men in his life, and I think that's important for him."

Dr. Kapp nodded toward Gramps and Xavier, heads bent over Gramps's cell phone. "Looks like he has one good male influence, at least."

"Yes, and I'm so thankful. But—"

"Tell you what," Dr. Kapp interrupted. "Why don't I take you down to see Ms. Hayashi? She's here now, setting up her classroom. I'm sure she'll be glad to talk to you about Xavier, and then if you're still feeling dissatisfied, we can talk. I know it's a special situation, but I just have a hunch that Ms. Hayashi is going to be the right placement for Xavier."

Troy parked the truck in the elementary school parking lot. Man, it felt good to be in the driver's seat again, but the doctor had been right about how he shouldn't drive. He could tell he was overdoing it. He used his crutches to make his way to the school's front door.

As he waited to be buzzed in, feelings from his past flooded him. The fun of going to school, the escape from the tension in his family, the relief of making new friends who didn't know anything about his big fancy home. He started to walk into the office when he saw

Angelica, her grandfather and Xavier following—could that be Kapp the cop, still running this place?—around a corner in the brightly painted hallway ahead, and he followed them. "Hey, sorry to be late."

"He's gonna be my dad!" Xavier said proudly to the school principal.

Troy's heart constricted at the boy's trusting comment. What had he, Troy, done to deserve that affection and trust? Nothing, but there it was, and it got to him. Made him want to earn it by being a really good dad to Xavier.

"Some say he always was the boy's dad," Gramps muttered, frowning at Troy.

Troy's fist clenched. Homer Camden was even older than Dr. Kapp, but someday he was going to get Troy put in jail for assault on a senior citizen.

"Gramps!" Angelica hissed, nodding sideways at Xavier, who fortunately had darted over to the wall to examine a fire alarm.

As the principal walked over to explain the fire alarm and caution Xavier never to pull it unless there was a fire, Camden glared at Troy. "Just saying what I've heard around town," he said in a lower voice.

Troy glared back. What an idiot. "If you want to talk to me about something, we'll talk later where the boy won't hear."

"Let's do that." He muttered, "Sorry" to Angelica as he walked over to study the fire alarm with Xavier and the principal.

"How's Bull?" Angelica asked. "Is he going to be okay?"

"Yeah, did you bring him with you?" Back at Angelica's side, Xavier wrapped his arms around his mom's legs and looked worriedly up at Troy.

Troy hesitated. "He's…he's not doing that well. He might need another operation. He's staying at the office in town for now."

"Oh no!" Xavier's eyes filled with tears. "He's gonna have to get his leg cut off and it's my fault!"

Immediately Troy squatted down, barely stabilizing himself on one crutch, his bad leg awkwardly out in front. "If Bull's leg has to be amputated, we'll do everything we can to help him do okay with it. Most dogs are just fine with three legs. There's even a special name for three-legged dogs."

"What is it?"

"Tripod," he said, tapping his palm with three fingers of his other hand. "See? One, two, three."

"I have to talk to Ms. Hayashi," Angelica said. "Do you think—"

Troy got it. "Hey, buddy," he said to Xavier as he shoved himself painfully to his feet. "What do you think about seeing the gym and the lunchroom first? Let Mom talk to your new teacher, and then we'll come back and look around the classroom. Okay?"

"Sure!" Xavier reached up and gripped Troy's hand where it rested on the handle of his crutch.

Troy looked at Homer Camden, red-faced and frowning, and for a split second, he got the image of a man who didn't know what to do with his feelings, who was jealous of a new man in Xavier's and Angelica's life, and who wanted only the best for them. He sighed. "Want to come along?"

Thank you, Angelica mouthed to him before disappearing into the classroom.

"Guess I can," Homer Camden groused. "If you can't handle the boy alone."

It was going to be a long half hour. But he'd do it for

Angelica. He'd do almost anything for her, if she'd let him, even though he wasn't at all sure that was wise.

"Where's the lunchroom?" Xavier asked as the three of them headed down the hall.

"Straight down thataway," Camden said, pointing, before Troy could answer.

"Wait a minute," Troy said, "did you go to this school, too?"

Camden nodded. "I was a member of the first graduating class. Back then, it was the new K-eight building, and I was here for seventh and eighth grade."

"That's cool, Gramps!" Xavier grabbed the older man's hand and swung his arms between the two of them, practically pulling Troy off his crutches.

"Back in those days," Camden said, "a lot of farm kids only finished eighth grade, so it truly was a graduation."

"What about you?" Troy had never thought about the old man's schooling, or lack thereof.

"Oh, I finished high school," Gramps said, a note of pride in his voice. "I was always good at math and science. English, not so much."

"Me, too," Troy said as they entered the school lunchroom, where a summer of cleaning couldn't quite erase the smell of sour milk and peanut butter. "That's why vet school had more appeal than, say, lawyering."

"But don't get too friendly," Gramps said as Xavier ran around looking at the colorful posters and sitting in various chairs. "I want to know why you're taking such an interest in Angelica and her son. Is there something you want to tell me?"

"Well, you know about our engagement." He felt duplicitous still, talking about something that might not happen. But it might. He was willing to marry Angelica and be a father to Xavier; he'd meant it when he'd offered, and he would stick with it.

"Is that because you're Xavier's dad?" Camden asked bluntly.

Troy stopped, turned and faced the other man. "No. I don't know who Xavier's father is. I'd like to, but so far, Angelica hasn't been willing to tell me."

Camden studied him. "I'm supposed to believe that? When you were engaged and spending practically every evening together?"

"It's not up to me what you believe," Troy said, "but it's the truth. Angelica and I had decided to wait until marriage." He couldn't keep the bitterness out of his voice. "Why she decided to change that plan, and with whom, I have no idea. But it wasn't me."

Camden crossed his arms over his chest and shook his head. "Guessin' that don't sit right," he said finally. "I always thought it was you. Thought you'd gotten her pregnant and then sent her away. But when you said you were marrying her now, you really threw me off."

Troy drew in a breath. "So you don't know what happened, who the father is?" He knew he shouldn't probe, should only discuss this with Angelica, but it felt like important information, and she wouldn't tell him. Maybe if he knew...

Camden shook his head. "Can't help you there."

"Come see this, Gramps!" Xavier was calling, and the two of them headed over just in time to stop him from squirting an entire container of ketchup into the sink. Plenty had gotten onto his shirt and shorts as well, and the two of them looked at each other with guilty expressions, obviously thinking the same thing: *we're going to be in trouble with Angelica.* A few paper towels later, they headed toward the gym.

"Do you know how to play basketball, Mr. Troy?"

"I sure do. I used to play at this school."

"Were you that tall then?"

Troy laughed. "No, son. I wasn't very tall at all."

"He was a pip-squeak. A lot smaller than you. I remember him in those days."

That hadn't occurred to Troy before, that Homer Camden had known him as a kid. On a whim, Troy put down his crutches. Camden grabbed a basketball, and they took turns lifting Xavier up to shoot baskets.

When they headed back toward the classroom, Xavier rested his hand on Troy's crutch again.

Which made Troy feel that all was right with the world. When had this boy put such a hold on his heart, enough to make him even see the good in Homer Camden?

When Xavier walked into the classroom between Troy and Gramps, tears sprang to Angelica's eyes. It felt as if all of her dreams were coming true.

She'd always wished her son could have a real father. And she'd hoped he could go to a regular school. It hadn't happened for kindergarten, because of all of his treatments, so this was his first opportunity.

"Hey, cool!" Xavier ran into the room and sat down at one of the desks. "I'm ready!"

"And is your name Sammy?" asked Ms. Hayashi.

Angelica was pretty sure she liked this teacher, who turned out to be the friend who'd come to the kennel with Daisy. She seemed very knowledgeable about children with medical issues, and her educational background was impeccable.

Her tight jeans, Harley-Davidson T-shirt and biker boots weren't everyone's idea of a first-grade teacher, even one who was at the school early to move books and set up her classroom. From Gramps's raised eyebrows, she could tell he thought the same. Angelica hoped the woman wouldn't intimidate Xavier.

But her son put his hands on his hips and spoke right up. "I'm not Sammy, I'm Xavier!"

"Aha. And do you know what letter your name starts with?" The woman squatted effortlessly in front of Xavier.

Xavier nodded eagerly. "An X, and I can write it, too!"

His enthusiasm made Angelica smile. They'd been practicing letters for months, and she'd taught him to write his name, but it had taken quite a while. His treatment had caused some cognitive issues that might or might not go away, according to the various nurses and social workers they'd dealt with.

"That's good. Can you find your desk?"

"How can I…"

The woman put a hand to her lips, took Xavier's hand and pointed to the sign on the front of the desk where he'd been sitting. "See? It's Ssssammy," she said, emphasizing the *S*. "What we need to do is to find your desk, the one that says "Xavier."

He frowned and nodded. "With an *X*."

"Yes, like this." She held her fingers crossed.

Xavier did the same with his hands. "I remember. Your nails are cool. I like purple."

"Me, too. Let's find that *X*."

So far, the woman hadn't even said hello to Troy or Gramps, but Angelica didn't care. She was impressed by Ms. Hayashi's educational focus and by how much learning was already taking place.

If only her son would remain healthy enough to benefit from it.

He'd woken up with a fever several mornings this week, which filled her with the starkest terror. Fear of relapse stalked every parent of a cancer kid. But, according to Dr. Lewis, all they could do was wait and see.

"Come see my new desk, Mr. Troy!"

Troy limped over, and Angelica followed, her arm around Gramps. Who didn't look as disgruntled as he had looked before. As Xavier showed with pride how the desk opened and closed, and Troy pretended amazement over the schoolbooks inside, Angelica snapped pictures and pondered.

She'd wanted Xavier to have a male role model. And maybe he already did.

Chapter Nine

Angelica was paying bills the next Saturday morning—thanking God for the job that allowed her to—when she heard a tapping on the door. Her heart did a double thump. Since she hadn't heard a car drive up, it had to be Troy.

They hadn't talked since their visit to Xavier's classroom and the closeness that had come out of that. She didn't know what to think of their up-and-down relationship. One minute he was mad at her about Buck, and then the next day he was acting like the sweetest father Xavier could possibly have, making her fall hard for him.

"Hey." Outlined in the early morning sunlight, his well-worn jeans and faded T-shirt made him look as young as when they'd been engaged. But now his shoulders bulged with the muscles of someone who ran a farm and lifted heavy animals and equipment. Running her hands up those arms, over his shoulders, as she'd done back then...it would feel totally different now.

"Hey yourself." When her words came out low, husky, she looked away and cleared her throat. "What's up? Everything okay at the kennels?"

He blinked. "The kennels are fine, but I wondered if you could help me with Bull." He nodded downward, and for the first time she realized that the bulldog was sitting patiently beside him, his wrinkly face framed by his recovery collar.

"Hey, big guy!" Feeling strangely warm, she knelt down to pet Bull, and he obligingly pushed up into a crooked standing position and wagged his stub of a tail.

"Is he okay?" She looked up at Troy. Man, was he handsome!

"He's doing pretty well. I can't tell for sure until the stitches are out, and it's time to do that. Then we'll see how he gets around."

He was saying it all without taking his eyes off her, and the intensity in his gaze seemed to be about more than the dog.

She looked down, focusing on Bull, feeling confused. Between her own feelings and the way Troy was looking at her, she was starting to feel as though they had an actual relationship.

Except they didn't. It was all about business and Xavier. Because if Troy knew the truth about her and her past and why she'd left, he'd never have anything to do with her. And what kind of relationship could you build on secrets and shame?

Back to business. "I need to get Xavier up and give him some breakfast," she said. "When were you thinking?"

He shrugged. "Whenever."

Something about the way he said it made her think of him rattling around his big house. Weekends could be so lonely when you were single. She knew it well, but at least she'd always had Xavier. "Would you…would you want to have breakfast with us first? I can make us something."

His face lit up. "Sure would. I'm strictly a cold cereal guy when I'm trusting my own cooking, but I do like breakfast food."

"Pancakes are my specialty." She didn't add that there'd been many nights when pancakes were all they could afford for dinner. "You go wake up Xavier. He'll love the surprise of it."

"Even better, how about if Bull and I wake him up together? We could probably even take the stitches out right here, if you don't mind my using your front porch as an exam room."

"Perfect." They smiled at each other as the sunlight came in the windows, their gazes connecting just a little too long. And then Angelica spun away and walked toward the kitchen, weak-kneed, her smile widening to where it almost hurt.

Half an hour later, she looked around the kitchen table and joy rose in her. Xavier was just starting to sprout a few patches of hair and his grin stretched wide. Troy sniffed appreciatively at the steaming platter of pancakes. Beneath the table, Bull sighed and flopped onto his side.

"Let's pray," she suggested, and they all took hands while Xavier recited a short blessing. Then she dished up pancakes and warm syrup to all of them.

"Delicious," Troy said around a mouthful.

"Mom's a good cook."

He swallowed. "Obviously." Then, a few bites later: "I'm impressed that you sit down at the table for meals and start them with prayer."

Angelica chuckled. "I could let you go on thinking we do that at every meal, but the truth is, there are plenty of nights when we eat off the coffee table and watch *Fresh Prince* reruns."

"Yeah, that's fun!" Xavier shoved another bite into his mouth.

"And we don't always remember to pray, either. I'm not a perfect mom *or* a perfect Christian."

Troy put a hand over hers. "Perfectly imperfect."

Yeah, if only you knew.

Later, Troy went and got his exam bag and then called Bull out to the porch, putting his crutches aside and lifting the dog down the hard-to-maneuver step. In every painstaking move, she saw his care for the old bulldog.

She got Xavier involved in a new video game, then went outside and petted Bull while Troy gathered his materials for removing stitches. "Hey, buddy, you gonna get your fancy collar off, huh?"

As if answering her, Bull pawed at the recovery collar that formed a huge bell around his neck.

"I'm going to try him without it," Troy said. "It's been driving him crazy, and he can't get around that well with it on. Depends on whether he'll leave the leg alone."

He put his hand on the dog and turned to her. "Angelica, I have to apologize."

She tipped her head to the side. "For what?"

"For going off on you that day. You were right. This guy wouldn't have survived without my having Buck to help me. I owe you."

She lifted an eyebrow. "You *were* quick to judge."

"I know. And I'm sorry. I'm kind of a Neanderthal where you're concerned." He looked at her with a possessive intensity that flooded her with warmth.

Troy had grown, for sure. He could see when he was

wrong and apologize. And he definitely had a softer heart these days. It looked as if he was blinking back tears when he gazed down at his old dog.

She didn't dare focus on what else his words evoked in her.

Troy removed Bull's stitches with skilled hands while she held the dog's head still and murmured soothing words. But as Troy examined the dog's leg more carefully, moving it back and forth, he frowned. "The range of movement isn't good," he said. "This is what my buddy the specialist warned me about. Once he starts to walk on it, I'm worried what will happen."

"Is there anything we can do?"

"Not right now," he said, still moving Bull's leg, intensely focused. "We'll have to watch him for a few more days, see how he does when he's free to move around."

After the stitches were removed, Angelica insisted on carrying Bull back to Troy's house. She'd noticed how badly Troy was limping, and it wouldn't do for him to ditch his crutches and carry Bull himself.

As she knelt beside Bull's crate, helping the dog settle in and petting him, Troy came up behind her and put a hand on her shoulder. After an initial flinch, she relaxed into his touch. Which felt amazing.

"So you were right about getting Buck's help and I was wrong," he said. "But I'm right about something else. Will you listen to me?"

She kept petting Bull, superaware of Troy's hand on her shoulder. "Okay."

"I want to take Xavier to a new doctor for his physical tomorrow."

She let go of Bull and scooted around to look at Troy. "What?"

"I found a new doctor for Xavier," he repeated. "We scored big-time. Great cancer doctor, hard to get, but he's an old friend of mine from college so I called in a favor. He's at the Cleveland Clinic, just about an hour and fifteen minutes away."

Before she could analyze her own response, it was out of her mouth. "No."

"What?" He looked startled.

"He likes the doctor we've started seeing here. I'd rather go to him. Anyway, it's just a simple physical for school and sports." She stood. "And I have to get back to Xavier."

He grabbed his crutches and held the door for her. "I'll walk with you if you'll listen."

"I listened. And then I said no." She started walking back toward the bunkhouse.

He followed. "Angelica, this is a really good doctor. Someone who specializes in leukemia."

"No."

"Wait." He turned toward her, leaning on his crutches, and looked hard into her eyes. "Why not? Why really?"

She looked away from his intensity. Why didn't she want a great new cancer doctor for Xavier? She took in a deep breath and started walking again. "Because I'm scared."

He fell into step beside her. "Of what? It can only be good for Xavier."

She stared at the hard dirt beneath their feet. "What if this doesn't work out?"

"What are you talking about?"

She glanced over at him. The morning they'd spent together, the delight of Xavier's happiness, of Troy's appreciation for her cooking, all of it made this so hard to say. "Look, I know the chances of us—you and me, this so-called engagement—making it are fifty-fifty at best. So what if we don't? What if you decide you don't want to go through with the marriage, or even if we do go through with it, that you don't want to stay? What are Xavier and I supposed to do then?"

He stared at her and then, slowly, shook his head. "You don't trust me, do you?"

"It's not you necessarily." She shrugged. "But why would you stick with us? What's in it for you? People don't just do things out of the goodness of their hearts."

They'd reached the bunkhouse porch, and he waited while she climbed the steps, then hopped up behind her. "What world have you been living in? Around here, people do things to help others all the time."

"Sure, give them a ride or watch their dog when they go on vacation. But marry someone? Stand by a kid with serious health issues? That's way, way beyond the call of duty, Troy. I appreciate your willingness, and for Xavier's sake, I have to give it a try. But—"

He tugged her down onto the porch swing and then sat next to her, held out a hand to touch her chin, ran his thumb ever so lightly over her lips. "Really? It's just for Xavier's sake?"

She stared at him, willing herself to stay still and explore the mix of feelings that his touch evoked. But she couldn't handle it. She scooted away and stood, and at a safe distance, pacing, she switched back to a safer topic. "Xavier hates changing doctors. If our relationship doesn't work, I certainly can't afford a fancy specialist. So that's why I'd rather just stick with the doctor we've been going to since we moved here."

"So you'd rather go with safe and mediocre."

"Dr. Lewis comes highly recommended," she protested.

"By whom?"

"Gramps and his friends." At his expression, she flared up. "I know you don't like Gramps, but he's been in the area forever, and all of his friends have medical issues, as does he. They know doctors."

"Geriatric doctors, not pediatricians. Look, this is a great opportunity. He'll get the athletic physical times ten. We're really blessed to see this guy, Ange."

Ange. It was what he'd called her when they were engaged, and hearing it thrust her back to that time. His excitement did, too.

Back then, she would have joined in readily, would have shared his optimism; she'd have been eager to try something new and take a risk.

But now, given her life experiences since that time, her stomach clenched. "I think Dr. Lewis will be just fine."

"Not really." He was getting serious now, leaning in, crossing his arms. "I asked around about Dr. Lewis. He's been in practice forty years. He isn't likely to be up on the latest research."

Angelica's spine stiffened and she felt her face getting hot. "I researched all the CHIP-eligible doctors within fifty miles. He's by far the best of those."

"Of those." His tone had gone gentle. "I'm not questioning that you did the best you could—"

"He seems really experienced. And Xavier liked him when we went when we first arrived in town."

He sighed. "Look, I just don't understand why you're not excited about this. It's a chance for your son to have the very best care around. Don't you want that?"

"Of course I do," she said, forcing herself not to

strangle the guy. "But listen, would you? It's hard for Xavier to handle a new doctor. He's suffered through a lot of them. I don't want to make a change when it might not be permanent."

He leaned over and clamped a hand on her forearm. "I'm not going to fall through. I'm here for you!"

She stared at him, meeting his eyes, trying to read them. But something about his expression took her breath away and she pulled free and turned to look out over the fields, biting her lip.

God, what do I do?

She wanted to trust Troy. She wanted to trust God, and hadn't she been praying for better medical treatment? Hadn't she had her own issues with Dr. Lewis's wait-and-see attitude?

Xavier banged out the front door, sporting a T-shirt Angelica hadn't seen before, and she pulled him toward her, hands on shoulders, to read it.

Rescue River Midget Soccer.

"Where'd you get this, buddy?"

He smiled winningly. "Becka gave it to me. It's her old one. But she said I can get a new one as soon as I'm 'ficial on the team."

Angelica's heart gave a little thump as she put her arms around him, noticing he was warm and sweaty. He must have been running around inside.

He wanted this so badly, and she did, too. But she worried about whether it was the right thing to do.

Here Troy was offering her an opportunity to get the best medical opinion, even on something so minor as whether a six-year-old could play soccer. Shouldn't she be grateful, and thanking God, rather than trying to escape their good fortune?

Even if it poked at her pride?

She took a deep breath. "Guess what! Mr. Troy found us a new doctor for you, a really good one. We're going to get you a super soccer checkup, to make sure you're ready to do your best."

The next day at the clinic, watching his friend and expert cancer doctor, Ravi Verma, examine Xavier's records and latest test results, Troy heaved a sigh of relief.

He had to admire the way Angelica was handling this. He knew he'd gone beyond the boundaries when he pulled strings to make the appointment, but he just couldn't stand to think that they were making do with a small-town doctor when the best medical care in the world was just another hour's drive away.

Obviously Angelica hadn't loved his approach, but she wasn't taking it out on Xavier. She'd pep-talked him through today's blood tests and played what seemed like a million games of tic-tac-toe as a distraction. Now she had an arm around her son as he leaned against her side.

She was a great mom. She was also gorgeous, her hair curlier than she usually wore it and tumbling over her shoulders, her sleeveless dress revealing shapely bronzed arms and legs.

Troy swallowed and shifted in his plastic chair. Man, this consultation room was small. And warm.

The doctor cleared his throat and turned to them. "There's so much that looks good on his chart and in the testing," he said, "but I'm afraid his blasts are up just a little."

"No!" Angelica's hand flew to her mouth, her eyes suddenly wide and desperate.

Troy pounded his fist on his knee. Just when things had been going so well. "What does that mean, Ravi?"

His friend held up a hand. "Maybe nothing, and I can see why my colleague Dr. Lewis wanted to wait—"

"He didn't even tell us about it!" Angelica sounded anguished.

"And that's common. The impulse not to alarm the patient about what might be a normal fluctuation."

"Might be…or might be something else?" Angelica's throat was working, and he saw her taking breath after breath, obviously trying to calm herself down. She stroked Xavier's back with one hand; her other hand gripped the chair arm with white knuckles. "What can we do about it?"

Ravi nodded. "Let's talk about possibilities. The first, of course, is to wait and see."

"Let's do that." Xavier buried his head in Angelica's skirt. He sounded miserable.

"Other options?" Troy heard the brusqueness in his own voice, but he couldn't seem to control his tone. Hadn't had the practice Angelica had.

"There is an experimental treatment for this kind of…probable relapse."

Angelica's shoulders slumped. "Probable relapse?"

Ravi's dark eyes flashed sympathy. "I'm afraid so. You see, his numbers have crept up again since his last test. Not much at all, so not necessarily significant, but from what I have seen in these cases…" He reached out and put a hand on Angelica's. "I think it might be best to treat it aggressively."

"Treat it how?" Angelica's voice was hoarse, and Troy could hear the tears right at the edge of it.

Xavier looked up at his mother. "Mom?"

"We'll figure it out, buddy." She smiled down reassuringly and stroked his hair with one hand. The other dug into the chair's upholstery so hard it looked as if she was about to rip it.

"The traditional protocol is radiation and chemo, quite intensive and quite…challenging on the patient."

Angelica pressed her lips together.

Troy leaned forward. "Is there another option?"

"Yes, the experimental treatment I mentioned. Cell therapy. Using the body's own immunological cells. Now, most of the participants in the trial are adults, but there is one other child, a girl of about twelve. It's possible I could talk my colleagues into allowing Xavier in, if he passes the tests."

"Isn't that going to be really expensive? We don't have good insurance."

"In an experimental trial, the patient's medications are fully funded. However…" He looked up at Angelica. "There may be some expenses not covered by our grant or your insurance."

"That's not a problem," Troy said. "Is this new treatment what you'd recommend?" he pressed.

Ravi looked at Xavier's bent head with eyes full of compassion. "If he were one of my own, this is the approach I would take."

Angelica opened her mouth and then closed it again. Shut her eyes briefly, and then turned back to Ravi. "How difficult is the treatment?"

"That is the wonder of it. It is noninvasive and not harmful as far as cancer treatments go because it uses the body's own cells. Of course, there are the usual tests and injections…" He reached down and patted Xavier's shoulder. "Nothing about cancer is easy for a child."

"I don't want a treatment." Xavier's head lifted to look at his mother. "I want to play soccer."

She lifted him into her lap and clasped him close. "I know, buddy. I want that, too."

Troy leaned toward the pair, not sure whether to touch Xavier or not. In the mysteries of sick children, he was a rank beginner. He had to bow to the expertise of Ravi, and especially of Angelica. At most, he was a mentor and a friend to the boy. "Buddy, this could make you well."

"It never did before." Xavier's expression held more discouragement than looked right on that sweet face. "Mom, I don't want a treatment."

"We'll talk about it and think about it. And pray about it." She straightened her back and squared her shoulders and Troy watched, impressed, as she took control of the situation. "Listen, I think Mr. Troy is feeling worried. And I also think I have a bag of chocolate candy in my purse. Could you get him some?"

Xavier sniffed and nodded and reached for her purse. She let him dig in it, watching him with the most intense expression of love and fierce care that he'd ever seen on a woman's face.

"Here it is!"

"Give Mr. Troy the first choice." She took back the purse and reached in herself, pulling out a creased sheet of paper. While Xavier fumbled through the bag of candy, patently ignoring her instruction to let Troy go first, Angelica skimmed down a list and started pelting Ravi with questions.

Troy imagined he could see the sweat and tears of their history with cancer on that well-worn paper. He didn't pray often enough, but now he thanked God for allowing him the honor of helping Angelica cope.

He focused on Xavier for a few minutes while the other two talked, bandying about terms and phrases he'd not heard even with his vet school history. Finally Angelica folded the paper back up, glanced over at Xavier and frowned. "Is there time for me to think about this?"

"Of course," Ravi said, "but it's best to get started early, before his numbers go up too high. If there is any chance you'll be interested in participating, we should start the paperwork now."

She closed her eyes for a moment, drew in a slow breath and then opened her eyes and nodded. "Let's do it."

During the little flurry of activity that followed—forms to fill out, a visit from the office manager to pin down times and details, some protests from Xavier—Troy kept noticing Angelica's strength, her fierceness and her decision-making power. She'd grown so much since he knew her last, and while he'd been aware of it before, he was even more so now. She had his total respect.

And she deserved a break. When Xavier's protests turned into crying and the office manager started talking about initial tests that would be costly but not covered by the trial's grant, he nudged the boy toward her. "Why don't you two go out and get some fresh air, maybe hit the park across the street? I need to talk to my friend here for a minute. And I'll settle up some of the financial details with the office manager and then come on out."

"Can we go, Mom?"

She pressed her lips together and then nodded. "I'll be in touch," she said to Ravi. She mouthed a thank-you to Troy, and then the two of them left.

Troy stood, too, knowing his friend's time was valuable, but Ravi gestured him back into the chair. "You cannot escape without telling me about her."

"She's…pretty special. And so is the boy."

"I see that." Ravi nodded. "They've not had an easy road, I can tell from the charts. Lots of free clinics, lots of delays."

"Has it affected the outcome?"

"No, I think not. It has just been hard on both of them."

"What are his chances of getting into the trial?"

"Honestly? Fifty-fifty. We have to look more deeply into all his previous treatments and his other options. But I will do my best."

"Thank you." And Troy made a promise to himself: he *would* make sure they got in. And, God willing, the treatment would make Xavier well.

That night, Angelica was helping Lou Ann clean up the kitchen—they'd all eaten together again—while Troy and Xavier sat in the den building something complicated out of LEGO blocks. The sound of the two of them laughing was a pleasant, quiet backdrop to the clattering of pots and dishes, and Angelica didn't know she was sighing until Lou Ann called her on it. "What's going on in your mind, kiddo?"

Angelica smiled at the older woman. "I'm just… wishing this could go on forever."

"Which part? With Xavier, or with Troy?"

"Both."

"Xavier we pray about. Is there a problem with your engagement we should take to the Lord, too?"

Lou Ann didn't know that the engagement was for show, and normally Angelica felt that was right and would have continued the deception. But something in the older woman's sharp eyes told her that she'd guessed the truth. "Yes," she said slowly, "we could use some prayer. I just don't know that it will work, not really."

"Why's that?" Lou Ann carried the roaster over to the sink and started scrubbing it.

Angelica wiped at the counter aimlessly. "Well, because I...I don't know, I just don't believe it can happen."

Lou Ann shook her head. "Why the two of you can't see what's under your noses, that you love each other, I don't know."

"We don't love each other!" And then Angelica's hand flew to her mouth. If the fact that their engagement was a sham hadn't been out before, it was now.

"I think you have more feelings than you realize," the older woman said. "So what's holding you back, really?"

Angelica leaned against the counter, abandoning all pretense of working. "I...I just don't believe he'll love me. Don't believe I'm able to keep him."

"The man's crazy about you!"

Lou Ann's automatic, obviously sincere response made Angelica's breath catch. "You really think so?"

"Yep."

Lou Ann's certainty felt amazing, but Angelica couldn't let herself trust it. "That's because he doesn't know much about me. If he did, he'd feel differently."

Lou Ann pointed at her with the scrubber stick. "What did you do that's so all-fired awful?"

Angelica shook her head. "Nothing. I...I can't talk about it."

"If it's about Xavier's daddy," Lou Ann said with her usual shrewdness, "I think you should let it go. The past is the past."

"Not when you have a child by it," Angelica murmured, starting to scrub again.

"Look," Lou Ann said, "all of us have sinned. Every single one. If you'd look at the inside of my soul, it would be as stained and dirty as this greasy old pan."

"You? No way!"

"You'd be surprised," Lou Ann said. "For one thing, I wasn't always as old and wrinkled as I am now. I had my days of running around. Ask your grandfather sometime."

Angelica laughed. "Gramps already told me you were the belle of the high school ball. In fact, I think he has a crush on you still."

Lou Ann's cheeks turned a pretty shade of pink. "I doubt that. But the point is, we've all done things we're not proud of. I ran around with too many boys in my younger days, and I've also done my share of gossiping and coveting. Not to mention that I don't love my neighbor as well as I should."

When Angelica tried to protest, Lou Ann held out a hand. "Point is, we're all like that. We've all sinned and fallen short, that one—" she pointed the scrubber toward the den where Troy was "—included. So don't go thinking your sins, whatever they are, make you worse than anyone else. Without Jesus, we'd all be on the same sinking ship."

"I guess," Angelica said doubtfully. She knew that was doctrine, and in her head she pretty much believed it. In her heart, though, where it mattered, she felt worse than other people.

"I think you need to sit down and talk to the man," Lou Ann said. "The two of you spend all your time with Xavier, and you don't ever get any couple time to grow your relationship and get to know each other."

"But our connection…well, you've pretty much guessed that it's mainly about Xavier."

"But it shouldn't be," Lou Ann said firmly. "You two should build your own bond first, like putting on your oxygen mask in a plane before you help your kid. If Mom and Dad aren't happy, the kids won't be happy. Xavier needs to see that you two have a stable, committed relationship. That's what will help him."

Angelica sighed. "You're probably right." She'd been thinking about it a lot: the fact that their pretend engagement had grown out of their control and was now of a size to need some tending. Half the town knew they were engaged, and more important, her own feelings had grown beyond pretend to real. She didn't want to think about ending the engagement, partly because of what it would do to Xavier, but also because of what it would do to her.

"You need to get to know him as he is now, not just the way he was seven years ago. Things have changed. He writes articles in veterinary journals now, and other vets come to consult with him. He's way too busy. And on the home front, his dad's not getting any younger, and Troy needs to make his peace with him. You're the one with the big, immediate issues in the form of that special boy in there, but Troy has his own problems to solve. You need to figure out if you can help him do that."

"Sit down. Take a break." Angelica nudged Lou Ann aside and reached for the scrubber, attacking the worst of the pots and pans. "I've been selfish, haven't I?"

"Not at all. You're preoccupied, and that makes sense. But promise you'll talk to him soon. Maybe even tell him some of that history that's got you feeling so down on yourself."

Angelica sighed. The thought of bringing up their engagement, of having that difficult talk, seemed overwhelming, but she could tell Lou Ann wasn't going to let it go. "All right," she said. "I'll try."

Chapter Ten

Angelica strolled toward the field beside the barn, more relaxed than she had felt in a week.

She'd tried to work up the courage to talk to Troy about their relationship, even to tell him the truth about why she'd left him, but it hadn't happened. Finally this morning, she'd turned the whole thing over to God. If He wanted her to talk to Troy, He had to open up the opportunity, because she couldn't do it on her own strength.

Red-winged blackbirds trilled and wild roses added a sweet note to the usual farm fragrances of hay and the neighboring cattle. Beyond the barn, she could hear boys shouting and dogs barking as Troy's Kennel Kids tossed balls for the dogs.

Today—praise the Lord—she'd gotten word that Xavier was accepted into the clinical trial. He'd go for his treatment in a couple of days, and Dr. Ravi was reassuring about everything. The treatment wouldn't be difficult, and he was optimistic that the trial would work, told stories of patients' numbers improving and "positive preliminary findings."

Impulsively she lifted her hands to the sky, feeling the breeze kiss her arms. *Lord, thank You, thank You.*

She rounded the corner of the barn and froze.

One of the Kennel Kids, older and at least twice Xavier's size, loomed over him, fist raised threateningly.

"Hey!" Poised to run to her son, she felt a restraining hand on her shoulder.

"Let him try to handle it himself," Troy said.

She yanked away. "He can't fight that kid! Look at the size difference!"

"Just watch." Troy's voice was still mild, but there was a note of command that halted her. "Wendell always pulls his punches, so don't worry."

Clenching her fist, still primed to run to her son, she paused.

Xavier smiled up guilelessly at the other boy. "Hey, I'm sorry my ball hit you. My pitching stinks."

"Leave him alone, Wendell. He's just a kid." One of the other boys put an arm around Xavier.

The bigger boy drew in a breath, and then his fisted hand dropped. "Yeah, well, don't hit me again. Or else."

One of the puppies jumped into the mix, and as if no threat had ever existed, the group broke into a kaleidoscope of colorful balls and yipping puppies and running boys.

As her adrenaline slowly dissipated, Angelica leaned against the wall of the barn and sank down to a sitting position.

"I want to go give Wendell some positive feedback. He's getting better about controlling his anger."

"I'm still working on that myself," she snapped at him, but halfheartedly. She knew it was good for Xavier to socialize with other kids, but these rough-around-the-edges boys scared her.

She watched Troy walk over and speak briefly with Wendell and then clap him on the back. Xavier, completely unmoved by his near brush with getting the tar kicked out of him, was rolling with one of the puppies.

Taking deep breaths, she willed herself to calm down. She hated the way Troy was high-handed with her, but after all, he was right, wasn't he? Xavier had handled the situation himself just fine and was fitting in nicely with the other boys. If she'd run in to save him, that might not be the case.

A few minutes later, Troy came back and sat down beside her. "You mad at me?"

"Yes and no." She watched as one of the other boys threw a ball back and forth with Xavier. The other boy was older; in fact, most of the boys were, but Xavier was holding his own. It reminded her of what a good athlete he could be.

If he got the chance.

And that was where Troy had been incredibly, incredibly helpful. "Listen," she said. "I don't necessarily like being told how to mother my kid, but there are times when you're right." She smiled up at him. "Dr. Ravi called today."

Troy's head jerked toward her, his face lighting up. "And?"

"And Xavier gets into the trial."

"That's fantastic!" He threw his arms around her.

No, no, no. She couldn't breathe, couldn't survive, couldn't stand it. She pushed hard at his brawny chest.

"Hey, fine, sorry!" He dropped his arms immediately and scooted backward, his eyebrows shooting up.

She gulped air. "It's fine. I'm sorry. I just…" Blinking

rapidly, she came back from remembered darkness—
something she'd had years of practice at doing—and
offered Troy a shaky smile. "I'm so grateful that you
made us see Dr. Ravi. He's wonderful. And I like that
he's going forward aggressively with the treatment. I
really, really want Xavier to have it. This could make
all the difference."

"I'm glad." Troy continued to look a little puzzled.
"But you're still mad at me?"

Mad wasn't the word. She knew she should launch
into the talk she'd promised Lou Ann she'd have with
Troy. She looked out across the fields and breathed
deeply of the farm-scented air.

And changed the subject. "Look, I know I'm overprotective. It kind of comes with the territory of parenting a seriously ill child."

"Of course."

"And I was worried about that bigger kid hitting him.
Xavier tends to bruise and bleed easily, or he did when
he was in active disease. I try to make sure he doesn't
fall a lot and all that."

"Should I have stopped them? I struggle with how
much to intervene and how much to let them work it out
themselves so they can build better social skills." He
studied his hands, clasped between his upraised knees.
"Thing is, a lot of these boys are out on their own much
of the time. I spend such a small fraction of their lives
with them. So I feel like they need to practice solving
some of their conflicts themselves. We usually talk it
over in group, after they've gotten some of their energy out." He shrugged. "I'm just a vet with a heart to
help kids. I don't know sometimes if I'm doing it right."

"You do a great job," she said warmly.

"Thanks." And then he was looking at her again, and

she spoke nervously to make the moment pass. "Parenting is like that for me. I never know if there's something I should do differently. Xavier's going to go to school, and he'll have to learn to handle the playground himself. I won't be there to intervene for him, so I guess that's something I'd better get used to."

"We can help each other out. We're a good partnership." He reached out and squeezed her shoulder.

She cringed away instinctively. And when she saw the hurt look on his face, she felt awful.

She opened her mouth to apologize and then closed it again. What was she going to say? How could she explain?

Nervously she pulled a bandanna out of her pocket and wiped off her suddenly sweaty neck and face. The thing was, she didn't know if she was going to get over this, ever. Being touched was hard for her. Oh, she could hug Xavier, did that all the time, and his childish affection was a balm to her spirit. When she stayed with Aunt Dot right after being assaulted, and indeed for years afterward until that wonderful woman had died a year ago, they'd shared hugs galore. And her girlfriends were always hugging on her and plenty of nurses had let her weep in their arms.

Female nurses.

It was only when a man hugged her that she freaked out.

Troy was regarding her seriously. His blue eyes showed hurt and some anger, too. "Look, I'm sorry," he said. "I guess I didn't realize how much you... Well, how much you don't want me near you. That's a problem. How are we..." He broke off, got awkwardly to his feet, favoring his hurt leg. "I better go check on the boys."

He limped off and she wanted to call him back, to apologize, to say she'd work on it, really she would. But the thing was, it had been seven years and she still wasn't over the assault.

She hadn't been motivated to get over it before because she hadn't dated anyone and she hadn't wanted a man around.

But Troy was doing so much for them. Moreover, when he touched her, she felt something uncurl within her, and that as much as anything made her shy away.

There'd been plenty of chemistry between them when they were engaged. Now, though, everything felt different.

She stared absently out at cornfields with tassels almost head high. Above her, the sky shone deep blue with puffy clouds.

She'd seen a counselor right along with her obstetrician, at her aunt's insistence, and the woman had been wonderful and had helped her a lot. But Angelica hadn't wanted to date. Hadn't wanted to open herself up to love—and the accompanying dangers and risks—again.

Still didn't, if the truth be told. She'd rather stay in her safe, comfortable little shell. But Troy was so good with Xavier, and Xavier needed a dad. Holding back like this was selfish of her. She had to fix this.

If she wanted to love again, a part of loving was hugging and kissing and all the intimate physicality created by the same God who'd made the corn and the sky and the sweaty little boys and jumping, bounding dogs in front of her.

She let her head drop into her hands. *Lord, I can't do this myself. Please help me heal. Help me learn to love.*

Slowly, as she listened for God's voice, as she breathed in the wonders of His creation, she felt herself relaxing. She didn't know if it would work for her. She certainly didn't want to tell Troy the reasons for her pain, because she knew he would judge her.

But maybe God would give her a pass on that. Maybe He'd let her have this relationship and let Xavier have a dad—a dad who could do amazing things with his connections, who could actually help Xavier heal—and she wouldn't have to tell Troy the sordid side of her past. Wouldn't have to tell him about her own culpability in what had happened to her.

Because no matter what her therapist had said, Angelica knew the truth. She'd gotten drunk and silly and flirty, and she'd been mad at Troy for not coming out to celebrate her birthday, and she'd been flattered when a handsome older man wanted to walk her home.

It wasn't pretty and it wasn't nice, and she'd regret it for the rest of her life.

God in His amazing excellence had turned it to good. God had brought her Xavier and he was the purpose of her life now, the thing that gave it meaning. And she, flawed as she was, loved him as fiercely as any mother could love any child, despite his bad beginning. God had done that much for them, overlooking her sins.

She could only hope and pray that He'd heal her enough to let her go forward with the marriage to Troy.

Troy strode away from Angelica and out toward the driveway. He just needed a minute to himself.

Apparently, though, he wasn't going to get it, because heading toward him was a police cruiser. Like any red-blooded American male who'd occasionally driven faster than he should, he tensed...until he realized that Dion was at the wheel.

Even seeing his friend didn't make him smile as he walked up to the driver's-side window.

"What's wrong with you, old man?"

Troy shrugged. He'd talk to Dion about almost anything, they were those kinds of friends, but there was a time and a place. "What brings you out my way? You're working nights. You should be home catching Zs."

"Yeah, had an issue." Dion jerked his head toward the backseat and lowered the rear window.

There, on a towel, was the saddest-looking white pit bull Troy had ever seen. Ears down, cringing against the backseat, quivering, skin and bones.

Troy's heart twisted.

"Found her chained to an abandoned house. You got your work cut out for you with this one."

Troy opened the rear car door and wasn't really surprised when the dog shrank against the back of the seat and bared her teeth. "Problem is, I've got the Kennel Kids here today."

"I know you do. I'm gonna help out for a bit while you take care of this little mama. Those boys could use an hour with a cop who's not out to arrest them."

Troy focused in on the word *mama*. "She's pregnant?"

"Oh yeah. It rains, it pours."

Troy drew in a breath and let it out in a sigh. "Okay. Lemme run get a crate and—"

Shaking his head, Dion turned off the engine and got out. "Can't crate her, man. She freaks."

"How'd you get her into the cruiser?" As always, when there was a hurting animal nearby, Troy went into superfocus, forgetting everything else, trying to figure out how to help it. He braced his hands on the car roof and leaned in, studying the dog.

Dion gave his trademark low chuckle. "One of the guys had a sandwich left over from lunch."

"Gotcha. Be right back."

Minutes later, with the help of a piece of chicken, the dog was out of the cruiser and in one of the runs right beside where the boys were playing.

"See what you can do, my man," Dion said, then strode over to the group of boys in the field, who went silent at the sight of the tall, dark-skinned man in full uniform.

Troy watched for a minute. Angelica was with them, and he saw her greet Dion. The two of them spoke, and then Dion squatted down to pet one of the dogs.

A couple of the boys came closer. Dion greeted them and apparently made some kind of a joke, because the boys laughed.

So that would be okay. Dion was great with kids; in fact, some of these boys probably knew him pretty well already, though not for as innocent a reason as his visit here today.

Using treats, Troy tried to get the dog to relax and come to him, but she cowered as far away as possible. From this distance, he could see her distended belly and swollen teats. She'd probably give birth in a week or two.

Xavier, for one, would be excited. He loved the puppies best, and though he was having a blast with the ones already here, watching them grow and playing with them, new babies would thrill him beyond belief. For that reason, Troy was glad they had a mama dog, though he had to wonder about this one's story.

Right on schedule, his sister pulled into the driveway. She helped with the Kennel Kids whenever she could.

"C'mere, Lily." On an impulse he named the dog for

her white coat, even if she was more gray than white at the moment. He threw a treat to within a few inches of her nose, and she made several moves toward it, then jerked back. Finally she dove far enough forward to grab the dog biscuit and retreat, and he praised her lavishly. Still when he moved toward her, she backed away, growling.

He settled in, back against the fence, watching the boys, Dion, Angelica and his sister.

Dion said something to Angelica and she laughed, and Troy felt a burning in his chest. Would Angelica go for his best friend?

A year older than Troy, Dion had been a little more suave with the ladies when they played football together in high school. But Troy had never felt jealous of the man…until this moment.

He tried to stifle the feeling, but that just made his heart rate go up, made him madder. Yeah, he was possessive, especially where Angelica was concerned. Nothing to be proud of, but the truth.

He watched Angelica and noticed that, while she was friendly to Dion, she kept a good few feet between them. Not like his sister, who often put an affectionate hand on Dion's arm or fist-bumped him after a joke.

Relief trickled in. Looked as though Angelica wasn't attracted.

He tossed another treat to the dog, and this time she dove for it and ate it immediately. He scooted a couple of feet closer, still staying low so he didn't look big and threatening to her. She let out a low growl but didn't attack.

He tossed another treat halfway between them, and the dog considered a moment, then crept forward to grab it.

He reached out toward the dog with a piece of food in his hand. This was a risk, as he might get bitten, but he figured it wasn't likely. He had a sense about this one. She wanted help.

A moment later, his instinct was rewarded when she accepted food out of his hand.

He fed her several more pieces and then reached toward her. She backed away, a low growl vibrating in her chest.

Righteous anger rose in him. He'd like to strangle the person who'd mistreated this sweet dog. Maybe ruined her for a home with a family. Fear did awful things to an animal.

Or a person.

It hit him like a two-by-four to the brain.

The dog was reacting the way Angelica reacted.

It was pretty obvious why, in the dog's case: people had treated her badly, and she'd learned to be afraid.

So who'd been mean to Angelica? What had they done? And when?

He jumped up, moved toward the dog and she lunged at him, teeth bared. He backed away immediately. He should know better than to approach a scared dog when he was feeling this agitated; she could sense it.

Had Angelica been abused or attacked?

No, not possible. He spun around and marched over to the kennels, grabbed a water bowl for the dog, filled it.

He had no idea what had gone on in Angelica's life in the years they'd been apart. She could very well have gotten into a bad relationship. And given that she'd apparently been poor, she could have lived in bad areas where risks were high and safety wasn't guaranteed.

He needed to talk to his social-worker sister. He took

the water bowl back to the new dog's run and set it down, keeping a good distance from her. Then he beckoned to Daisy.

She came right over. "Hey, bro, what's happening with Xavier and Angelica? Did you find out about the cancer trial?"

"Xavier got in. We're pretty happy."

Hands on hips, she studied him. "Then what's eating you?"

"You know me too well. And you understand women, and I don't."

She raised her eyebrows. "What's up?"

He looked out at the cornfields. "If a woman was… abused, say, or attacked…how would she react? Wouldn't she tell people what happened?"

Daisy cocked her head to one side. "Probably, but maybe not. Why?"

"Why wouldn't she tell?"

"Well…"

He could see her social work training kick in as she thought about it.

"Sometimes women are ashamed. Sometimes their attacker threatens them. Sometimes they're in denial, or they just want to bury it."

He nodded. "Okay, it makes sense that they might not want to report it, to have it be common knowledge. But if they have close family or friends who would help them…"

"Are you talking about a rape?"

The word slammed into him. And the doors of his mind slammed shut. That couldn't have happened. Not to Angelica. *Please, God, no.*

Daisy crossed her arms over her chest and narrowed

her eyes at him. "Whatever you're thinking, you need to talk to that person about it. Not to me."

He nodded, because he couldn't speak.

"So go do it."

He drew in a breath, sighed it out. "Cone of silence?"

"Of course."

Slowly he walked over to where Dion leaned against a fence, talking to a rapt group of boys. Angelica knelt a short distance away beside the pen they'd made to keep Bull safe from too much activity but still included in the fun. She was rubbing the old dog's belly, praising him for how his leg was healing, telling him he'd feel better soon. She looked pensive and beautiful and she didn't hear him coming.

Deliberately he touched her shoulder, and just as he now expected, she jumped and frowned toward him.

He hated being right. "We have to talk," he said to her. "Soon."

Chapter Eleven

The next Saturday night, Angelica listened to the closing notes of the praise band and wished she felt the love the musicians had been singing about.

Sometime during the past month, coming to Saturday night services with Lou Ann, Troy and Xavier had become the highlight of her week. The focus on God's love, the sense of being part of a community of believers and the growing hope of a future here—all of it made church wonderful. But tonight, she'd been too jittery to enjoy it.

She felt Troy's gaze on her—again—and scooted toward the edge of the padded pew. "I've got to go get Xavier."

"No, that's okay." Lou Ann sidled past her and out of the pew. "I'll do it."

Oh. Rats.

Troy turned to greet the family next to them, and, hoping he hadn't heard her exchange with Lou Ann, she started edging out of the pew. Grabbing her purse, she stood and took a sideways step, then another.

Suddenly some kind of hook caught her wrist, and

she looked down to see the crook of a wooden cane tugging at her.

She spun back toward him. "Troy! What are you doing?"

"I knew this thing was good for something," he said, holding up the cane he'd borrowed from Lou Ann and offering her a repentant grin. Then he scanned the room. "The place is emptying out. We can have some privacy. Do you mind staying a minute?"

Yes, I mind! She bit her lip, shook her head and sank back down onto the pew. It was probably better to stay here in the sanctuary than to go off somewhere by themselves. Somewhere she might feel that strange sense in her stomach again, that sense of…

Being attracted.

Yeah, that.

She hadn't felt it for years—in fact, she hadn't felt it since she was engaged to Troy—and it was making her crazy.

"We've got to talk about why you jump every time I touch you."

"Don't open that can of worms, Troy," she said quickly. Of all their possible topics of conversation, that was the one she most wanted to avoid.

He cocked his head to one side, studying her face. "Actually we've got to talk about a few things," he said finally. "One of which is this marriage. People are asking more and more about it. We can't put them off forever with some vague engagement plans in the future."

Early-evening sunshine slanted through stained-glass windows, and the breeze through the church's open back door felt cool against Angelica's neck. "I know. It's Xavier, too. He wants to know when the wedding will be."

"Is there going to be a wedding?" He watched her, his face impassive.

Her heart skipped a beat. "Do you want to back out?"

"Noooooo," he said. "But I'm seeing some implications I wasn't thinking about before." Deliberately he reached out and took her hand.

It felt as if every nerve, every sensation in her body was concentrated in her hand. Concentrated to notice how his hand was bigger, more calloused than hers. To notice the warmth and protection of being completely wrapped in him. Waves of what felt like electricity crackled through her veins.

He was watching her. It seemed he was always watching her. "You feel it?"

Heat rose to her cheeks as she nodded.

"So…we're going to have to figure out what to do with that."

Somehow even admitting she felt something for him—something like physical attraction—made her feel panicky and ashamed. She looked away from him, focusing on the polished light wooden pews, on the simple altar at the front of the church. Her hand still burned, enclosed by his larger one, and she pulled it away, hiding it in the folds of her dress.

"It's not wrong, you know. It's a mutual thing, a gift from God, and He blesses it in the context of marriage." Troy's voice, though quiet, was sure.

Angelica wanted that quiet certainty so much. She wanted Troy's leadership in this area. Wanted to feel okay about her body and wanted to find the beauty in physical intimacy sanctioned by God. It had been so long since she felt anything but sadness and regret about the physical side of life. Here, in God's house, she wanted to hope. But did she dare? Was change possible after all these years? Could God bless her that much?

Xavier and Lou Ann came hurrying in through the side front door of the sanctuary. *Whew, relief.*

"Hey, you two." Lou Ann reached them right behind Xavier and leaned on the pew in front of them. "Some of the kids and parents are walking over to the Meadows for ice cream. Is it okay if I take Xavier along?"

"Please, Mom?" Xavier chimed in.

Angelica grabbed her purse. "I can take him," she said to Lou Ann.

"That's okay. I could use a rocky road ice-cream cone myself." Lou Ann reached over and put a hand on her shoulder, effectively holding her in the pew. She leaned down and whispered, "Besides, you need to talk to him."

"Do I have to?"

"Yes, you have to!" Lou Ann patted her arm. "I'll be praying for you."

"Thanks a lot!" She bit her lip and watched Lou Ann guide Xavier off, trying to remember what was most important: God was with her, always, and God forgave her, and God would help her get through this whole thing.

She drew in a breath, and the peace she'd been seeking during the service came rushing in. *Pneuma.* Holy Spirit. God.

She turned back to Troy and he took her hand again, and immediately that uncurling inside started. That opening; that vulnerability. She tried to pull away a little, but he held on. Not too tight, not forcing her, but letting her know he wanted to keep touching her.

Angelica let him do it, her eyes closed tight. She

didn't want to like his touch. Didn't want to need him. It would be so much easier and safer not to open up.

He tightened his grip on her hand, ever so slightly. "I want you to tell me why you pull away all the time."

"I'm not sure—"

"Hey, hey, the engaged couple!" Pastor Ricky came over and clapped Troy on the shoulder, leaned down to hug Angelica, overwhelming her. She shrank back, right into Troy. *Aack.*

"Have you two set a date yet? Are you wanting to get married here? You'd better reserve it now if you're planning to do it any time soon. We're a busy place."

"We were just talking about that," Troy said.

"Make an appointment with me to start some premarital counseling, too." He made a few more minutes of small talk and then turned to another pair of parishioners and walked away with them.

"He's right," Troy said. "We've got to decide."

"I know." But inside, turmoil reigned.

Xavier needed a dad in the worst way, and Troy was the perfect man for the job. The three of them were already close.

Xavier needed it, needed Troy, but she herself was terrified.

Lord, help me. Her heart rate accelerated to the pace of a hummingbird. She could barely breathe. She looked up at Troy, panicky.

"You can talk to me." He slid an arm along the back of the pew behind her, letting it rest ever so lightly around her shoulders. "What is it you need to tell me?"

She took deep, slow breaths. The fact that she was shaking had to be obvious to Troy.

What part could she tell him? What part did she need to keep private? What part would come back to bite her?

Tell him the worst right away.

Like yanking off a Band-Aid. She moved to the edge of the pew, away from his arm, and pulled her hand from his. Clenching her fists, she turned her head toward him, looking right at his handsome face. "I was…I was raped."

"Raped? What? When?"

It was the first time she'd ever said that word, even to herself. Her vision seemed to blur around the edges, bringing her focus to just his mouth, his eyes. She had to grip the edge of the pew, waiting for the expression of disgust and horror to cross his face.

His mouth twisted.

There it was, the anger she'd expected. She looked away from his face and down at his hands. His enormous hands. They clenched into fists.

She shrank away. Was he going to hit her right here and now? Frantically she looked around for help.

"Tell me." He sounded as though he was gritting his teeth. But his voice was quiet, and when she looked at his hands, they'd relaxed a little. He wasn't moving any closer, either.

"Troy, I'm sorry…I was drinking. I should have been more careful."

"Man, I'd like to kill the jerk who did that to you. When did it happen?" His voice was still angry, and she couldn't blame him. At least it was a controlled anger, so she wasn't at immediate risk.

Even though it would destroy their relationship, she'd started down this path and she had to keep going. *God, help me.* "It was…after my twenty-first birthday celebration. Remember I went out to that bar?" She heard the urgent sound in her voice. Couldn't seem to calm down.

His expression changed. "I remember that night. I had to work and couldn't go." He pounded a fist lightly against the pew. "I should have been there to take care of you."

"I was drinking."

He took her hand in his. "It's not your fault. Man, I wish I'd been there." He shook his head slowly back and forth, his eyes far away, as if he were reliving that time.

Not her fault? She looked away, bit her lip. That was what her therapist and her aunt had said, but she'd never really believed it. Could Troy?

"Look," he said, "as far as any physical connection between us is concerned, you can have all the time you need. I'll be patient. I understand."

Tears filled her eyes. Was it possible that, even knowing this, Troy could still want her?

"So…wait. That's when Xavier was conceived?"

She nodded, staring down at her lap, kneading her skirt between her hands. He was being kinder than she had any right to expect. She blinked and drew in shuddery breaths as tension released from her body.

Telling him the truth was something she'd barely considered at the time because she was terrified of what his reaction would be. She'd had some vague image of yelling and rage and judgment, and the notion of Troy, her beloved fiancé, doing that had pushed her right out of town. Better to leave than to face that pain.

He didn't seem to be blaming her. She could hardly believe in it, couldn't imagine that his kindness would stay, but even the edge of it warmed her heart.

"Who did it, Angelica?" Troy's voice grew low, urgent. "Was it someone you knew? Someone we knew?"

And there it was, the part she didn't dare tell him.

"Did we know him?" Troy repeated.

Still looking down at her lap, she shook her head. Did it count as a lie if she didn't say it out loud?

Troy looked at Angelica with his heart aching for all the pain she'd been through and his fists clenching with anger at the jerk who'd done this to her. He tried to ignore the tiny suspicion that she wasn't telling the whole truth.

His mother had constantly lied to his father. He didn't want to believe it of Angelica, but her body language, her voice, her facial expressions—all of it suggested she was keeping something from him. "We were engaged. You should have told me."

"I blamed myself," she said in a quiet voice. "And I knew how much my chastity meant to you."

Her words hit him like a physical blow. "You think that would be more important than taking care of you? I would've helped you."

"Out of obligation," she said, glancing up at him and then away. "But you wouldn't have liked it."

"Was I that kind of a jerk?" He didn't think so, but look how he was feeling right now. Compassion, sure, but with the slightest shred of doubt in his heart.

He grabbed the Bible from the rack in front of them and held it. For something to do with his hands, but also to remind himself to take the high road and think the best. "I can't believe this happened to you," he said, turning the Good Book over and over in his hands, thinking out loud. "It was a crime committed against you. It's not your fault, and you shouldn't blame yourself." He put the Bible down beside him. "And if you didn't report the crime then…" He searched her face, saw her shake her head, looking at her lap again. "If you didn't say anything already, you should now. The man should be brought to justice. I'll talk to Dion. He knows everything about the law."

"No!" She scooted away from him, an expression of horror on her face. "I don't want to dig into it again. And anyway, it's not…it's not necessary."

"We gotta get the guy! Don't you want justice?"

She shook her head. "No. I don't want anything to do with the police."

"Are you protecting someone?"

"I just don't want to get the police involved. For all kinds of reasons."

Why wouldn't she tell him who did it? Was she telling the truth, that she didn't know the person?

And if she was lying, then how much did she really care for him?

He looked at her face and was shocked by the disappointment he saw there. Immediately he felt awful. She needed support, she needed help. She needed a dad for Xavier, and speaking of that sweet kid…wow, he was the product of an assault. And she'd mothered him despite that, wonderfully.

Whatever mistakes she'd made in the past, he was going to provide what he could for her. He reached out to put his arm around her. Felt her stiffen, but remain still, letting him do it.

There was none of the tender promise of before, though. There was more of a cringe. He reached out involuntarily to stroke her shiny hair.

She pulled away and stood. "I'm going to leave you to think about this. It's a lot to take in, I know."

"Angelica—"

"We'll talk later, okay?" Her lips twisted and she hurried off toward the back of the sanctuary.

Leaving him to his dark thoughts and guilt and anger, a mixture that didn't seem to belong in this holy place.

Chapter Twelve

"I'm terrified," Angelica admitted to Lou Ann as they dug carrots from the garden. "They hated me before and they'll hate me even more now."

The older woman shifted her gardening stool to the next row. "Troy's family isn't that bad."

Hot sun warmed Angelica's head and bare arms, and the garden smells of dirt and tomato vines and marigolds tickled her nose. Around them, rows of green were starting to reveal the fruit of the season: red tomatoes, yellow squash, purple eggplant.

Later today, she and Troy and Xavier were going to join his family at the small country club's Labor Day picnic. Just the words *country club* made Angelica shudder.

Not only that, but her relationship with Troy had felt strained ever since last Saturday, when she'd revealed the truth about how Xavier was conceived. Although he'd responded better than she'd expected, she still felt questions in his eyes every time he looked at her. It made her want to avoid him, but they'd had the plan to go to the Labor Day picnic for weeks.

And she had to see whether she could stand it and

whether his family could accept Xavier. Had to see whether to go forward with the marriage or run as fast as she could in the opposite direction.

The older woman sat back on her gardening stool. "You put way too much stock in what those people think."

"What they think about me isn't that important," Angelica said, "but I don't want them to reject Xavier."

Lou Ann used the back of her hand to push gray curls out of her eyes. "I've yet to meet a person who could dislike that child. What God didn't give him in health, He gave him double in charm."

"Which he knows how to use," Angelica said wryly. "But what he doesn't know is which fork to pick up at what time. I don't, either. We've neither of us ever been to a country club."

"He never took you when you were engaged?" Lou Ann asked, and when Angelica shook her head, the other woman waved a dismissive hand. "Honey, this isn't some ritzy East Coast place. This is a picnic in small-town Ohio. I've been to the country club dozens of times. It's just a golf course with a pool and some tennis courts. Ordinary people go there."

"People like me? I don't think so." She remembered the girls from high school who spent their summers at the club. They wore their perfect tans and tennis whites around town as status symbols. Angelica could only pretend not to see their sneers as she scooped their ice cream or rang up their snack purchases, working summers at the local Shop Star Market.

"You've got the wrong idea," Lou Ann said. "Rescue River's country club has always been a welcoming place. Never had a color barrier, never dug into your marital status, never turned away families based on their religion. They're open to anybody who can pay the fee, which isn't all that much these days. I've thought about joining just to have a nice place to swim."

Angelica tugged at a stubborn weed. "You may be right, but Troy's family can't stand me. Not only did I dump their son, but my grandfather threw a wrench in their plans to dominate the county with their giant farm. We've been feuding from way back."

"Isn't it time that ended?" Lou Ann pulled radishes while she spoke. "The Lord wants us to be forces of reconciliation. I know Troy believes in that. You should, too."

Angelica sat back in the grass, listening to crickets chirping as a breeze rustled the leaves of an oak tree nearby. God's peace. She smiled at Lou Ann. "You're my hero, you know that? I want to be you when I grow up."

"Oh, go on." Lou Ann's flush of pleasure belied her dismissive words.

"But I'm still scared."

"You know what Pastor Ricky would say. God doesn't give us a spirit of fear, but of power and love and self-control."

"Yeah." Angelica tried to feel it. Sometimes, more and more often these days, she felt God's strength and peace inside her.

But this Labor Day picnic had put her into a tailspin. Steaks and burgers weren't the only thing likely to be grilled; she would be, too.

"Here's a little tip," Lou Ann said. "Pretend like they're people from another country, another culture. You're a representative of your culture, bringing your own special gifts. You're not expecting to be the same as them, just to visit. Like you're an ambassador to a foreign land."

Angelica cocked her head to one side, her fingers stilling in the warm, loose dirt. Slowly a smile came to her face. "That's a nice idea. If I'm an ambassador, I'm not under pressure to be just like them."

"Right. You just have to think, that's interesting, that's not how we do it in my culture, but that's okay."

"Yes! And in my culture, we'd bring a gift." Angelica reached for a sugar snap pea and popped it into her mouth, savoring the vegetable's sweet crunch.

Lou Ann smiled. "Atta girl. What would you bring?"

"Food, probably. But that's the last thing they need, especially at a country club bash."

Lou Ann tugged at a recalcitrant carrot and then held it up triumphantly. "Anyone would welcome fresh vegetables from a garden."

Angelica flashed forward to imagine herself and Xavier walking onto the country club grounds. The image improved when she threw in a basket of zucchini, tomatoes and carrots. She threw her arms around the older woman. "You're a genius!"

Troy pulled up to the bunkhouse and, on an impulse, tooted the horn in the same pattern he used when he'd dated Angelica years ago. It was a joke, because he'd always insisted on coming to the door even though she urged him not to. It used to be something of a race, with him hustling to get out of his car and up to the door before she could grab her things and burst outside.

He couldn't beat her now, though. By the time he'd grabbed his stupid cane and edged gingerly out of the truck—man, his leg ached today—Angelica had emerged from the bunkhouse. Her rolled-up jeans fit her like a dream, and her tanned, toned arms rocked the basket she was carrying, and Troy wanted to wrap his arms around her, she looked so cute.

"What do you have there?" Troy asked. He was proud of her, proud of bringing her to meet his family. Remeet them, actually; they'd all known each other forever. But Angelica was a different person now, and they all had a different relationship.

"Just a little something for your dad."

"For Dad, huh?" Troy tried to smile, but he wondered how that would be received. His father was notoriously difficult, and Troy had already warned Angelica that his dad's moodiness had gotten worse. None of them could go a whole evening without causing him to yell or cuss or storm out of the house.

Lou Ann came out bringing Xavier, fresh-scrubbed and grinning.

Troy gave him a high five. "You ready for some fun, buddy? They have a blow-up bounce house and a ball pit and face painting."

"Face painting is for girls," Xavier said scornfully.

"I just now saw your outfit," Lou Ann said to Angelica, then turned to Troy. "Have they changed their rules about denim?"

Angelica's face fell. "Aren't you supposed to wear jeans?"

"It's no problem," Troy said. "They did away with that rule a couple of years ago."

"I didn't even think of it," Angelica said uneasily.

He put a protective arm around her shoulder. "You'll be fine. You look great!" But the truth was, he was on edge himself. It wasn't just his dad's bad moods; his older brother wasn't much better. Dad and Samuel, the two wealthiest men in the community, could be an intimidating pair.

"It'll be fine," he repeated. And hoped it was true.

When they got to the club, they were greeted with the smell of steaks and burgers grilling and the sound of a brass quartet playing patriotic songs. The whole place was set up like a carnival, with music and clowns and inflatables, and kids ran in small packs from one attraction to the next.

"This is so cool, Mom!" Xavier's eyes were wide, as if he'd never seen anything like this before. And knowing how poor they'd been, maybe he hadn't.

"It really is." She was a little wide-eyed herself.

He took Xavier by one hand and Angelica by the other and urged them forward. "We'll find you someone fun to play with," he told Xavier. "Samuel's girl, Mindy."

"A girl?"

"Girls can be fun!" He squeezed Angelica's hand, trying to help her relax, and looked around for his brother's daughter. Truthfully he worried about the girl. With an overprotective, suspicious father who tended to stay isolated, she often seemed lonely. "Hey, Sam!" He waved to his brother, gestured him over.

Sam walked toward them, frowning, holding Mindy's hand.

"Hey," Troy greeted his brother, glaring to remind him to be polite. "You remember Angelica, right?"

Sam gave him a quick nod and turned to Angelica. "Angelica. It's been a long time."

"And this is Xavier, Angelica's son."

"Say hello," she prompted gently.

But Xavier was staring at Mindy. "What happened to your other hand?"

"Xavier!" Angelica sounded mortified.

"I was born without it," Mindy said matter-of-factly. "What happened to your hair?"

"Leukemia, but it's gonna be gone soon and then I'll have hair."

Mindy nodded. "Want to go see the ball pit? It's cool."

"Sure!" And they were off.

"I'm so sorry he said that," Angelica said to his brother. "He should know better."

"No problem," Sam said, but to Troy's experienced ear, the irritation in his brother's voice was evident. He hated for anyone to comment on his daughter's disability. Plus, the man was frazzled; since his wife's death, he'd had his hands full trying to run his business empire and care for his daughter.

"Kids will be kids," Troy said as a general reminder to everybody, especially his brother.

"That's true," Sam said. "I'm sorry Mindy commented on your son's hair. Are things going okay with his treatment?"

"I'm hopeful," Angelica said quietly. "Lots of people are praying for him."

They strolled behind the two running children. Troy kept putting his arm around Angelica while trying not to actually touch her. He was being an idiot, but there'd been awkwardness between them ever since their botched conversation the other night, when she told him about her attack. He wished he hadn't pushed her to reveal her assailant, but he wanted to know because the guy deserved punishment. He also needed to be off the street.

Xavier and Mindy were chattering away as they zigzagged from craft table to ball toss. The adults, on the other hand, were too quiet. "Angelica brought some vegetables for Dad," Troy told Sam, trying to keep this reunion from being a total fail.

His brother nodded. "Too bad Dad hates vegetables."

"Oh." Angelica's face fell. "They're fresh from the garden back at Troy's house. I've been helping Lou Ann take care of it. Does he even hate fresh tomatoes?"

"Pretty much. But," Sam added grudgingly, "his doctor told him he needs to eat better, so maybe this will help."

"We made some zucchini bread, too. Maybe he'll like that, at least."

"I'm sure he will," Troy said firmly.

Sam didn't answer, and after a raised-eyebrow glance at him, Angelica shrugged and got very busy with examining the Popsicle-stick crafts at the kids' stand and checking out the tissue-paper flowers some of the older girls were making. The brass quintet started playing old-fashioned songs, of the "Camptown Races" sort, and the smell of grilled sausage and onions grew stronger, making Troy's mouth water.

"Where's Dad?" he asked to kill the awkward silence.

"I'll get him," Sam said. "Watch Mindy, would you?"

"Sure."

As Sam left, Angelica looked up at Troy. "He hates me. I can tell."

"Well, he doesn't *hate* you. He doesn't hate anyone. He's a good guy underneath. But he's had people take advantage of him a lot, and his wife's death was really traumatic. So bear with him. He's protective of his family, and he thinks you hurt me."

"I did hurt you," she said softly. After a minute's hesitation, she reached out and lightly grasped his forearm, and the touch seemed to travel straight to his heart. "I never apologized about that. I shouldn't have left like I did, Troy. I should have trusted you more, and it was wrong of me to leave without any explanation. You can maybe understand how desperate I was, but still, I realize now that it was a mistake."

"Thanks for saying that." Seven years later, he found that the apology still mattered. His throat tightened. "I appreciate hearing those words from you. But I'm sorry, too."

"For what?" She looked up at him through her long lashes, and she was so pretty he just wanted to grab her into his arms. But you didn't do that with Angelica.

"For being the type of person who'd judge a woman for something that wasn't her fault." He saw Mindy stumble, watched Xavier reach out a hand to steady her. "Life's taught me not to be so rigid about everything."

"Isn't that the truth?" She laughed a little, looking off toward the cornfields in the distance. "We all learn as we get older."

"Well, most of us." He nudged her and nodded toward his father, who was being urged out of his seat by Sam and Daisy. "Some are a little more thickheaded and it takes longer."

"Here we go," she said, obviously trying to be funny, but he could hear the dread in her voice.

"Just don't let anything he says get to you. I've got your back."

"Thanks." She tightened her grip on his arm and then let go. Today was the first time Angelica had initiated touching him since they met again, and he had to hope that it meant there was some promise for them together.

Xavier and Mindy shouted for them, and they turned to watch the two kids skim down the inflatable slide together. Around them, people were starting to gather at tables covered by checkered tablecloths. Parents were trying to get their kids to come to supper, helped along by the smell of hot dogs and cotton candy.

The warm sun and music and patriotic decorations brought back memories of his parents in happier days, of playing baseball and Frisbee with his brother and sister here at the club, of eating and laughing together before everything had started to go wrong in his family.

Behind them, he heard his father's grousing voice. "I don't want to walk all the way over there. I just got comfortable sitting down and—"

"Come on, Dad." It was Daisy, and when he turned to look he saw that she was urging their father along by herself; Sam had apparently bailed on supervising this meeting. "Troy's fiancée is here," Daisy continued determinedly, "and you need to welcome her. Hi, Angelica!"

Angelica offered a big smile. "It's good to see you, Daisy. Hi, Mr. Hinton."

"Hello." His father didn't say anything rude, thankfully; that probably meant he hadn't had much to drink yet. But he looked Angelica up and down with a frown.

"Dad, Angelica brought you some vegetables from the garden."

She rolled her eyes at him, subtly, and he realized he was trying too hard.

"Humph." His father looked at the basket dismissively. "Green stuff."

Troy opened his mouth to smooth things over, but Angelica took a step in front of him, effectively nudging him out of her way. "Sam said you don't like vegetables, but there's some zucchini bread I made from

Lou Ann Miller's recipe. I hope you like it." She held
out the basket.

"Thank you." His father took it begrudgingly. "That
woman always won the prize at picnics when we were
teenagers. Even back then, she was a good cook."

Angelica smiled. "She still is. Maybe you could come
visit sometime."

Troy gritted his teeth. He avoided inviting his dad
over because the man was so difficult. He didn't like
what Troy was doing with his life—being a vet, especially doing rescue. The Hinton sons should be making
money hand over fist in the world of agricultural high
finance, according to his dad.

"So you've taken to being a hostess at Troy's house,
have you?" his father asked.

"Dad!" Daisy scolded before Troy could intervene.
"Angelica has every right. She's marrying Troy."

As Angelica followed the group toward the long din-
ing tables, Daisy's words rang in her ears like chimes
foretelling her fate. *"She's marrying Troy."*

"Hi, Angelica!" A blonde in spike-heeled sandals approached, with mirror-image blond girls holding each
hand. Ugh. She'd wanted a distraction, but not necessarily in the form of Nora Templeton—one of the country-
club girls who'd been meanest when they were in high
school together. Was her voice really prissy? Or was
Angelica just defensive?

"Hi, Nora," she said, holding out a hand.

"Let Mommy shake hands, Stella," Nora said, pulling loose from one of her daughters to hold out a perfectly manicured hand.

Which made Angelica wonder if she'd gotten all the

dirt out from under her own nails since her marathon gardening session that morning.

"Run along and play a minute." Nora shooed her daughters away. "How are you? I heard you were back in town."

"Yes." As Nora's daughters high-fived each other and ran off toward the dessert table, Angelica debated how much to tell. "My son and I wanted to spend more time with my grandpa."

"That's sweet. I see your grandpa sometimes at the Towers when I visit my aunt." She leaned closer. "Your son looks a lot like his daddy."

Angelica's world blurred as she stared at the other woman. Did Nora know Jeremy, her assailant, then? Who else did?

"He's got that same dark hair and sweet smile."

Around them, people stood in clusters or found seats at family-sized tables. Troy's friend Dion was sitting down with an older couple, and he saw her and gave a friendly wave.

Angelica fought to stay in the present and analyze Nora's words. Did she mean Jeremy? Had Jeremy talked about what had happened, then, after threatening her with a worse assault if she ever said a word?

Nora's eyes grew round. "Did I say something wrong? I just assumed Troy's your son's father."

Angelica's breath whooshed out. Troy. Nora thought Troy was Xavier's dad.

"If it's supposed to be a secret, I won't say anything to anyone. But I think it's just so sweet that you two are finally getting married."

Angelica stared at the other woman blankly while her mind raced. Should she just let this happen, let the misperception remain? Was that fair to Troy? To Xavier?

"Mom! Stella rubbed cake in my face and we didn't even eat dinner yet!"

"Girls! Stop that!" Nora looked apologetically at Angelica. "They're not always such brats. See you around!" She rushed off, leaving Angelica in a haze of self-doubt.

Oh, she'd been stupid, thinking she could bring Xavier here to live without putting this small, close-knit community on alert. Everyone had to be doing the math in their heads, figuring out that Xavier was of an age to have been conceived during her former engagement to Troy.

"Come on, Angelica." Daisy's voice brought her back from the brink. "They're about ready to serve dinner, and Dad likes to be first in line."

"Make me sound like a cad," her father grumbled.

The savory tang of barbecue sauce and the slightly burned scent of kettle corn filled the air as they straggled toward long tables heaped with potato salad, watermelon and enormous silver chafing dishes of baked beans.

Lou Ann had been right: the crowd included all skin colors, just like the town. There was even a man wearing a turban at one table and a group of women in brightly colored saris at another. Cooks and servers in pristine white aprons and chefs' hats shouted instructions to one another, punctuated by the laughter of family groups and the shouts of children.

Angelica ran a hand over Xavier's bald head and felt the tiniest hint of stubble. A bubble of joy rose in her chest, reminding her of what was really important.

As Angelica helped Xavier load his plate for dinner, Troy's father stood next to her in line. "I told my son not to get together with you," he said in what was apparently supposed to be a whisper, but was probably audible to everyone up and down the long serving buffet.

"Oh?" Ignoring the stares and nudges around them, she scooped some baked ziti onto Xavier's plate. "Why's that?"

"Because you dumped him before," Mr. Hinton said. "Fool me once, shame on you, fool me twice, shame on me."

Heat rose to her cheeks, but she just nodded. What could she say? She had left Troy, it was true.

"What's that man talking about, Mom?" Xavier asked in a stage whisper.

"Ancient history," she said.

"Actually history about the same age as you are."

The server behind the grill was openly staring. "Shrimp or steak, ma'am?"

"Xavier," she said, "take this plate over where Mindy's sitting. I'll be right there."

As soon as Xavier left, she turned to Mr. Hinton, hands on hips. "Any issues you have with me, you're welcome to tell me. But don't involve my son. None of this is his fault, and he has a lot to deal with right now."

Mr. Hinton narrowed his eyes at her. "Your son is part of the issue. Is he related to me?"

She cocked her head to one side.

"I mean, is my son his father?"

Light dawned. "No, of course not! Troy would never…" She trailed off. Mr. Hinton believed that, too? She'd known on some level that acquaintances like Nora might think Xavier was Troy's son. But she was shocked to realize that his own father suspected it.

Keeping Xavier's parentage a secret was hurting Troy. But revealing it would hurt Xavier.

Lou Ann's words came back to her. As a Christian, she was supposed to be all about reconciliation.

She turned to Mr. Hinton, gently took his plate and put it down on the buffet table and nudged him off to the side, ignoring the raised eyebrows of family members and bystanders around them. She pulled him by the hand to a bench out of earshot of the crowd and sat down, patting the seat beside her.

He gave her a grouchy look and then sat.

Aware that she didn't have long before he left in a hissy fit, she talked fast. "Look, I can understand why you're upset with me. And I can understand why you want to know whether Xavier is a blood relative. The answer is no. He's not."

Mr. Hinton crossed his arms and glared at her. "All the more reason for me to be angry, then. Isn't that right? Isn't my son opening himself up to a lying, cheating woman by getting back together with you?"

His voice had risen and people were staring; conversations in the area had died down. She'd *thought* this area was secluded enough to keep their conversation private, but apparently, with the volume of Mr. Hinton's hard-of-hearing voice, it wasn't.

It was her worst nightmare come true: she was a spectacle at the country club, looked down on by the other guests.

What's the right thing to do, Lord? The prayer shot straight up through the tears that she couldn't keep from forming in her eyes.

An arm came around her shoulder, and Troy sat beside her, pulling her to his side. His strength held her up where she felt like collapsing.

"Dad," Daisy said as she hurried over to clutch her father's shoulder, leaning over him from the other side.

"Why are you making a scene? You know this isn't right."

"No." Angelica straightened her spine, pulled away from Troy, and stood. "He's not doing anything but protecting his son. That's totally understandable."

"Thank you!" Mr. Hinton's exasperated words almost made her smile.

"But, Mr. Hinton," she said, reaching out to clasp his arm. "That's what I need to do, too. Xavier's story is his own to tell, and he's too young to understand it and share it yet. So I'm just going to have to ask you to take it on faith that, when the time is right, you'll know the right amount about his parentage."

"That's about as convoluted as a story can get," Mr. Hinton complained, but his voice wasn't as loud and angry as it had been before.

"Dad. I know enough to understand what happened," Troy said. "None of it is Angelica's fault, and I'd just ask you to accept Xavier without any questions right now. That's what I'm planning to do."

"And that's what this family is about," Daisy said firmly. "We accept kids. All kids."

Angelica took deep breaths and shot up a prayer of thanks. Troy had supported her. And it looked as though Daisy was coming around to her side, too.

Mr. Hinton was a tougher case, but he was just trying to protect his child and his family. That was something she could understand.

"Come on," she said, and took the risk of clasping his hand. "Let's go get back in line before the food's all gone."

He cleared his throat. "Finally somebody said something that makes sense." As they walked together to the line, he leaned down to mutter in her ear, "You tell

Lou Ann that nothing on the dessert table here holds a candle to her zucchini bread."

"Wait. You've been sampling dessert already?"

"Life's short. Eat dessert first. Right?"

"I think I'm going to follow that philosophy," Angelica said, grabbing a big piece of chocolate cake.

"You're not my favorite person in the world," Mr. Hinton said to her. "But I reckon I can back off of hassling you. Xavier's not accountable for your problems. And come to think of it, you're not accountable for your grandfather's."

Angelica gave the old man a sidearm hug and then sidled away before he could either embrace her or reject her.

"Humph." He glared at her and bustled off.

It wasn't a warm welcome, but Angelica felt that progress had been made. And she shot up a prayer of thanks and wonder to God, who was clearly the author of the peace and reconciliation she'd just felt.

Chapter Thirteen

After dinner, they all moved over to sit near the band. Xavier was fighting tiredness, but losing the battle, so Angelica talked him into lying down for a little rest on the blanket beside her. He resisted, but in minutes, he was asleep.

The gentle music prompted a few older couples onto the makeshift dance floor, where moonlight illuminated them in a soft glow. Most of the younger kids were quieting down or already asleep, while the teenagers paired off at the edges of the crowd. Nearby, most of the Hintons were spreading blankets and settling in to listen to the music.

She wanted this for Xavier. She wanted the community and the family and the security represented by life here.

She'd never thought she could have it. When she left seven years ago, running scared, she'd thought her connection with this community was severed. Now she had a chance to regain it, stronger than when she was young, to regain it as part of a connected, loving family.

She wanted it so badly, but was she just setting herself up for disappointment?

"Aw, he's so sweet," Daisy said, coming over to settle in the grass beside her. "He got along really well with everyone, didn't he?"

"I was pleased. But he's a great kid that way. He's always had an ease and charm with people that I can only envy."

Daisy cocked her head to one side, studying Xavier. "I wonder where he gets that."

The comment echoed in Angelica's head. Where did Xavier get his charm and people skills?

The thought pushed her toward his genetics, toward Jeremy and his superficial charm, but she shoved that idea away. "My aunt helped out with him so much when he was small. She was an amazing woman, and I'm sure he picked up some of her better traits."

"I'm sure he's picked up some of your great traits," Daisy said, patting her knee. "I really admire what you've done, raising him even though…" She stopped.

"Even thought what?"

"Look," Daisy said, "I'm guessing Xavier is the product of some kind of an assault. Remember, I'm a social worker. I see stuff like this all the time. I can tell you're wary of men in a way that suggests you've been treated badly, and I know you didn't use to be like that, so…" She spread her hands expressively.

Angelica stared at the woman, feeling defeated. Daisy had guessed most of the story of her past. As much as Angelica wanted to hide it, it was written and apparent in the existence of Xavier.

"I'm sorry." Daisy patted Angelica's arm. "There I go blurting stuff out again. I should learn to put a sock in it."

Angelica let out a rueful sigh. "For sure, I don't want to talk about my past troubles. But am I going to be able to escape it? Is it wrong for me to want to keep it all private?"

"From me, it's okay," Daisy said. "I have no right to your private information. But I would think that Troy would want to know whatever information is available about Xavier's father."

"That's what I'm afraid of." Troy was the last person she wanted to tell. The trust developing between them was a beautiful thing, but fragile. Revealing the name of her attacker might downright destroy it. After all, Troy had looked up to Jeremy. Would he believe that a guy he admired, a guy who'd mentored him, who'd been a town athletic star, had done something so awful to Angelica?

Or would he turn on her instead?

"But maybe not," Daisy went on, lying back to stare up at the emerging stars. "Maybe he won't need to know. Troy is a rescuer at heart. He's taken in animals since he was a little kid, and in those cases you don't know what happened. But you deal with the results."

"Gee, thanks, Daisy." She whacked the woman on the calf, welcoming the distraction from her own uneasy thoughts. "Did you just compare me to a rescue dog?"

Daisy grinned. "If the shoe fits…"

"If the dog coat fits…" Angelica played along. She was glad that she and Daisy could joke. But what the woman had said bothered her. Why did Troy want to be with her, anyway? Why was he willing to put up with not knowing Xavier's background?

Was it because he saw her, not as an equal human being, but as a creature to be rescued?

"Today's the day, buddy!" Troy turned in the passenger seat to give Xavier a high five. "I get my cast off, and you get to start playing soccer on the team."

"Just to try it," Angelica warned as she swung the truck around the corner. "Remember, when we go to your checkup on Thursday, Dr. Ravi is going to let us know if soccer is the right thing for you to do."

Xavier's jaw jutted out, and Troy could almost see his decision to ignore his mom. He looked down, grabbed the soccer ball from the seat beside him and clutched it to his chest. "Hey, Mr. Troy, do you think you could be one of the coaches?"

"I don't know much about soccer, buddy." But the idea tickled his fancy. What a great way that would be to connect with Xavier. And to help kids. Coaches had been a huge part of his own childhood, giving him the encouragement his dad hadn't.

Xavier was bouncing up and down in the car seat. "You played football before. You could learn about soccer. Please?"

"We'll see, buddy. I have to get the okay from my doctor. Just like you."

"Really?" Xavier's eyes went round as quarters. "I didn't think grown-ups had any rules."

Troy and Angelica exchanged amused glances, and Troy reached back to pat Xavier's shoulder. "We have more rules than you know. And if we're smart, we follow the rules. We listen to doctors."

Xavier frowned and nodded, obviously thinking over this new concept.

Angelica flashed Troy a grateful smile as she pulled up to the door of the hospital. *Thanks*, she mouthed.

Looking at her made his heart catch fire. She was everything to him, and once he got this wretched cast off, he'd feel whole again and as if he could take control. She wouldn't have to drive him and he would be able to be a full partner to her and Xavier. They'd be able to set a wedding date and move forward with their lives, with a real marriage.

"Let me know if you need a ride when you're done."

"This should be pretty quick. Afterward, I'll just stroll over to the park and you guys should still be doing practice."

He gave in to a sudden urge, leaned over and dropped a kiss on her cheek. Her hair's fruity scent and the sound of her breathy little sigh made him want to linger, and only his awareness of Xavier in the backseat held him to propriety.

Especially when she didn't pull back.

He felt ten feet tall. They were making real progress as a couple. What a great day.

"What was that for?" she asked while Xavier giggled from the backseat.

"Just feeling good about everything."

He walked into the hospital easily, barely using his cane. After checking in and waiting impatiently in a roomful of people, the nurse put him in a room to wait for X-rays.

The technician came in and told Troy to hop up on the exam table. "First I'll cut the cast off and then we'll x-ray everything." He was bent over an electronic tablet, recording and filling things in. Finally he looked up. "Hey, I know you."

Troy studied the bearded man, who looked a little younger than Troy. "You do look a little familiar." Then it clicked into place: this was the man they'd seen outside the Senior Towers, that day they'd done the weeding. The one Angelica hadn't liked. His friend's younger brother.

"I'm Logan Filmore." He held out his name tag as if to prove it. "I was a couple years behind you in school, but I watched you play football with my brother."

"Right, right!" Troy reached out, shook the man's hand. "I'm sorry for your loss." Logan's brother had died in a car accident about five years ago. "The whole town came out for Jeremy's funeral. What a loss."

"Yeah." Logan frowned as he positioned Troy on the x-ray table. "I keep hearing that from everyone now that I've moved back permanently."

They made small talk as Logan took pictures of Troy's leg in every position. When the ordeal seemed to be almost over, Logan looked at Troy with a serious expression. "I hate to bring this up, but I heard that you're pretty intense with Angelica Camden. Is that true?"

"Yeah." Troy smiled to remember their exchange in the car. "In fact, we're getting married pretty soon."

"That's great." Logan moved the X-ray machine to another position. "Now, lie still for this one. It's a full 360 and takes a few minutes to get warmed up." He made a tiny adjustment to Troy's leg. "So, you feel okay about everything that happened before?"

Something in the man's tone made Troy's stomach clench. "What do you mean?"

"I mean, about her leaving town pregnant, staying away. You…" He shook his head. "I don't know if I could do that, raise another man's child."

Heat rose inside Troy but he tamped it down. "That's between me and Angelica. And anyway, a kid's a kid."

Logan took a step back, palms out like stop signs. "For sure. Didn't mean anything by it."

"No problem." He'd have to learn to deal with nosy people. It came with the territory of marrying a woman with a kid and a bit of mystery in her past.

"Anyway, I'm glad to see my nephew get a good home. After Jeremy passed, I always thought I should do something, but since Jeremy said she didn't want it…"

His *nephew*? Icy shock froze Troy's body. "Want what?"

"Well, any help with the baby. I guess she felt like, since it was just a one-night stand, he didn't owe her anything."

"Just a one-night stand." Troy repeated the words parrotlike, feeling about as dumb as an animal. "What do you mean? Are you saying Xavier is Jeremy's son?"

"Yeah. Oh man, didn't you know?" Logan's eyebrows shot up. "I thought sure she would've told you. Or you would've asked." He slapped the heel of his hand to his forehead. "Man, I feel like a fool. I'm sorry. What a way to find out."

Troy just lay there on his back under a giant machine, his heart pounding like sledgehammer blows, sweat dripping from his face into his ears. *He* was the one who felt like a fool.

"Okay, ready? Lie still now."

Troy forced himself to obey while the machine moved its slow path up and down his leg. Inside, anger licked slow flames through his body. It took massive self-control not to jump up and slug Logan, though none of this was his fault.

It wasn't Troy's fault, either, nor Xavier's.

It was Angelica's fault. Angelica, and the guy Troy had always looked up to, the guy who'd stayed after practice to help him when he was a scrawny freshman, the guy who'd argued his case when the coach thought Troy was too focused on his studies to play first string.

Troy's mind reeled. Angelica had called it a rape, and he'd 99 percent believed her. So why did Logan think Jeremy was Xavier's dad?

And why did he have details about Angelica not wanting Jeremy's help? Wouldn't she have wanted it?

Well, but if it had been a one-night stand…

Because Jeremy wouldn't rape anyone. Would he?

He felt as if a million little dwarves were hammering at his brain. He wanted out of this conversation. This room. This whole wretched situation.

"Why do you think Xavier is Jeremy's child?" he ground out after the infernal machine had done its work and Logan was back in the room, a sheaf of X-rays in hand.

"Because he told me." Logan crossed his arms over his chest, looking off into space. "Man, that was one of the last times I saw my brother, right before I went overseas. We were out drinking one night and got to talking. He told me they'd hooked up." Logan's gaze flickered down, and he must have seen the turmoil on Troy's face. "Oh man, I'm sorry to break that news. Especially to a guy who's having this kind of trouble with his leg."

"What?" What did his leg have to do with anything? Who cared about his leg now?

"Here, sit up. Take a look." Logan pinned Troy's X-rays up on a light board and pointed. "That didn't heal worth nothing, man. It's all wrong. I don't know if they'll rebreak it or just leave it." He studied the light board, cocking his head to one side. "I don't think I ever saw a break heal that bad before, dude. My sympathy." He went to the door. "Sit tight. Doc will be in any minute. And hey, sorry to be the bearer of bad news."

Angelica sat on the grass watching Xavier joyously joining in the soccer practice. She still felt a little out of place with the other parents, all of whom seemed to have known each other for years. People were friendly, but Angelica knew she was still an outsider. Had always been an outsider, even when she was a kid.

"Good kick, Xavier!" one of the other children yelled.

Coach Linda, Becka's mom, waved to her. "Your son's a natural! Hope he can stay on the team!"

She watched as her son, completely new to soccer, raced to the ball and took it down the field in short, perfect kicks. Or whatever you'd call it…dribbling, maybe? She was way short on soccer terminology.

She so wanted for Xavier to fit in, and truthfully she wanted to fit in with the community, too. During her early years with Xavier, scrambling with work and day care, sometimes struggling to find a place to live before she'd settled in with her aunt, she'd looked enviously at families watching their kids play sports, kids with not only parents but grandparents and aunts and uncles to cheer them on. Families that could afford the right uniforms, could get their kids private lessons or coaching. She'd never even had the chance to dream of such a thing for her and Xavier, but now, hesitantly, she was starting to hope it could happen. They could be a part of things. They could have love, and a community, and a future.

When Nora, the woman from the country club, came up to her with a clipboard, Angelica smiled at her, determined to keep her walls down, to make a fresh start. "Hi," she said, extending her hand. "Are your girls on the team? I'm hoping Xavier can join."

"I heard. He seems really good." The woman settled down on the bench beside Angelica. "I'm head of the parents' organization. We do fund-raising and plan the end-of-season banquet for the kids, so I wanted to get you involved."

Pleasure surged inside Angelica. "Great. I'm pretty new to all this, but I'm glad to help however I can."

"Let me get your contact information." Nora pulled out her iPhone.

As she punched in Angelica's address, she smiled. "So you're living with Troy already, are you?"

Angelica swallowed. *She doesn't mean anything by it. Don't take it personally.* "No, we're not living together exactly. Xavier and I live on the farm, in the guesthouse."

"Oh, I'm sorry! I just assumed, since you have the same address... Great job, Nora, foot in mouth as usual. Never mind."

"It's okay. I work at the kennels," Angelica said, hearing the stiffness in her own voice. "That's why we live there."

"Oh! I misunderstood." The woman leaned in confidingly. "You know, ever since I got divorced, people have been trying to match me up with Troy."

Angelica looked sideways at the woman's perfect haircut and designer shorts. She was tall with an hourglass figure. What had Troy thought of her? Had they gone out?

Nora waved her hand airily. "It didn't work out. He's a great guy, though."

"Yes, he is," Angelica said guardedly. Why hadn't it ever occurred to her that Troy had other options he was closing off by being involved with her? That he could date, or even marry, someone like Nora, the gorgeous, well-off, country-club-bred head of the parents' group?

"So, I notice Xavier doesn't have a uniform yet," the woman continued. "They cost fifty dollars. And we ask that parents make a donation of fifty dollars to the group, for parties and snacks and special events."

Angelica swallowed. "Um, okay. I might need to do one thing per paycheck, if that's okay. Money's a little tight."

The woman laughed. "You're kidding, right? Troy has all the money in the world."

I want to fit in, God, but do I have to be nice to this busybody? "Like I said, we'll take it one thing at a time. I'd like to get him the uniform first, but if you need the parents' fee right away—"

"Oh no, it's fine." The woman shrugged, palms up. "You pay when you're ready. Or when you tie the knot! I know Troy's good for it."

That rankled, and then another truth dawned as Angelica realized how her engagement to Troy must look to much of the town. Here she was, in her ancient cutoffs, and Xavier in his mismatched holey T-shirt and thrift-store gym shorts, and apparently Troy was known as one of the richest men in town. Just like when they'd been engaged before. They were two people from opposite sides of the tracks. They didn't fit.

Did everyone think she was marrying Troy for his money?

Angelica's phone buzzed, and when she saw Dr. Ravi's office number on the caller ID, she wrinkled her nose apologetically at Nora. "Sorry, I have to take this." When the woman didn't get up to move, Angelica stood and walked out of earshot. "Hello?"

"Angelica, it's Dr. Ravi. I got your message about Xavier playing soccer, and I wanted to tell you I think it's wonderful."

"Really? He's cleared to play?"

"Not only that, but all the signs about the treatment

are very, very positive. Of course, definitive cures aren't part of the language of cancer doctors, but we are looking at very, very good numbers."

"Oh, Dr. Ravi, thank you! That's wonderful!"

"I agree." In his voice, she could hear his sincere happiness. "One never likes to make promises, but if I were you, I would be planning a long, healthy future for that young man."

Angelica half walked, half skipped back to the bench and sat down, vaguely conscious that there were a couple of other moms there with Nora now. She couldn't even remember why she'd felt upset with Nora.

What an incredible gift from God. She looked up at the sky, grinning her gratitude. Wow, just wow. She felt like shouting.

"Could you give me your email and cell phone information for our parents' directory?" Nora was looking at her, eyebrows raised.

"Um, yes, I… You know what, can we do this later? I just got some really, really good medical news. Xavier! Hey, Zavey!"

Xavier came trotting over. "Mom, did you see me score a goal?"

She reached out widespread arms and caught him in them, holding him so tight that he started to struggle. Reluctantly she let him go but held his shoulders to look into his eyes. "Guess what?"

"Mom, can I go back and play more?"

Her smile felt so broad that her cheeks hurt. "You sure can. In fact, Dr. Ravi says you're cleared to play, and that the treatment seems to be working."

His eyes and his mouth both went wide and round. "You mean I'm getting well?"

"Looks like it, kiddo."

"And I can be on the team? And have my own shirt?"

"Absolutely. Just as soon as I get my next paycheck, you'll have a uniform, buddy."

He took off his hat and threw it high in the air, and the other moms seemed to draw in a collective sigh at the sight of his cancer-bald head.

"You know," Nora said, "I'm sure that, between us, we can get him a uniform right away. Can't we, ladies?"

The others nodded, and one of them, an acquaintance from years ago, reached out to give Angelica an impulsive hug. "We're so glad you moved back. It'll be great to get to know you again."

"Yes, and with Xavier playing, maybe our team will win a game every once in a while," chimed in one of the other moms, and they all laughed.

"Hey, there's Dad!" Xavier pointed down the street. "Can I go tell him, Mom? Can I?"

She was so happy that it didn't even bother her that Xavier had called Troy "Dad" in front of all these mothers, who, no matter how nice, were likely to gossip about it. She looked in the direction Xavier was pointing and saw Troy walking toward them, along the sidewalk. A part of her wanted to tell Troy the great news about Xavier herself, but she couldn't deny Xavier the delight of telling. After all, it was his news. "Go for it, honey. Just don't knock him down. He looks a little bit tired."

Angelica watched Xavier running toward Troy, soccer ball under one arm, and happiness flooded her heart. It almost seemed in slow motion, like a dream: she was surrounded by other moms who seemed, suddenly, like supportive friends. The warm, late-afternoon air kissed her cheeks, tinged with the scent of just-mown grass. Giant trees shaded them all, testimony to how long this park had been here, how deeply the community was grounded in history.

She wanted this, especially for Xavier, so much she could taste it. And here it was within their grasp.

Xavier got to Troy, shouting, "Mr. Troy! Dad! Guess what!"

Troy kept walking. Limping, actually, and he still had his cane.

Angelica's heart faltered.

"Mr. Troy, hey! Don't you hear me?" Xavier grabbed Troy's leg.

Troy stumbled a little.

Angelica sprang from the bench and strode toward them, ignoring the concerned exclamations of the other mothers.

"Hey, Mr. Troy, guess what!"

Finally Troy stopped and turned to Xavier. "What?" His voice was oddly flat.

"I can play soccer! And I'm gonna get all better!"

Knowing Troy so well, Angelica could see him pull his mind from whatever faraway place it had been. He turned and bent down awkwardly, slowly. "That's great news, buddy." He was clearly trying to show enthusiasm. Trying, and failing.

To which her excited son was oblivious. "So that means you can be my coach, right? Can you, Dad? Can you?"

"We could use a few extra coaches, Troy," Coach Linda called from among the group of mothers. "Hint, hint."

Troy looked toward them, forehead wrinkled, frowning. "No," he said. "No, I can't do that."

"Whaddya mean you can't, Dad? You gotta coach me! You said you would."

Angelica reached the pair then and, breathless, knelt down beside Xavier. "Give Mr. Troy a minute here, buddy." She studied Troy's face.

He was looking from her to Xavier with the strangest expression she'd ever seen. Eyes hooded, corners of his mouth turned down. She couldn't read it and for some reason, it scared her.

"What's wrong?" she asked, putting a protective arm around Xavier.

"Mr. Troy, watch what I learned already!" Xavier threw the soccer ball he'd been carrying up into the air and bounced it off his head. Then he dribbled it in a circle, then kicked it up into his hands again.

His ability to handle the ball took Angelica's breath away. He was well, or pretty close, and he was going to be able to develop this amazing talent. She clasped her hands to her chest, almost as if she could hold the joy inside.

"Don't you want to coach me now?"

Troy looked at the two of them for a minute more. Then, without another word, he turned and started limping toward the truck.

She felt Xavier's shoulders slump.

"Troy!" she said. "Come back here and tell us what's going on."

He didn't answer, didn't look at her, just kept walking. And now she could see that he had a pronounced limp from some new, big kind of bandage around his leg, beneath his long pants.

"Troy!" When he didn't answer, she put her hands on her son's shoulders. "Remember how tired and cranky you can get from going to the doctor?"

Xavier nodded. But his lower lip was wobbling. He was so vulnerable, and she could have kicked Troy right in his bad leg for hurting her son's feelings. "Well, I think that's how Mr. Troy is feeling now."

"Did he have a treatment?" Xavier asked. "Does he have cancer, like me?"

"He doesn't have cancer, but I think he must have had a treatment that hurt or something. So we'll talk to him later. Right now I think your team needs you." Gently, she turned him back toward the playing field. She waved to Coach Linda, ignoring the curious stares of the other mothers. "Hey, Coach, Xavier's coming back in to play some, okay?"

"We can use him," Linda called, and as Xavier ran toward her, she reached out an arm to put around his shoulders.

Angelica watched long enough to see the pair head back toward the field. Both of them glanced back a couple of times, Xavier still looking a little crestfallen.

She marched after Troy.

"Hey, what's going on?"

He didn't stop, but she caught up with him easily.

"Troy! What happened at the doctor's? Did you get bad news?"

He got to the truck and looked at it. Shut his eyes as though he was in physical pain. Then walked to the passenger door and opened it.

"Troy! I thought you... What happened?"

He closed the door and sat in the truck, staring straight ahead.

She reached out and pulled the door open before he could lock her out. "Look, I get that you've had some bad news, but let me in, okay? Tell me what's going on. We're a team, remember? We're engaged! We're getting married!"

"No, we're not."

The three words, spoken in that same flat tone he'd used with Xavier, pricked a hole in her anger. She felt her energy start to flow out of her, like a tire with a slow leak. "What do you mean? Talk to me."

He didn't.

"What happened? Why aren't we getting married now? Troy, no matter what happened to you, which I'd appreciate being told about, you can't just shut me out. And I don't like your ignoring Xavier that way. You really hurt his feelings."

"And of course I wouldn't want to hurt the feelings of Jeremy's son."

Jeremy's son.

A core of ice formed inside her. He knew. Troy knew the truth.

Jeremy's son.

She never thought of Xavier that way. Xavier was her son. God's son. Soon, she'd thought, he would be Troy's son.

Though Jeremy Filmore had had a role in his conception, a role she'd spent a lot of years blocking out, it had ended there.

Hearing Troy say that name made her feel like throwing up. She staggered and leaned against the side of the truck. It was hot, but somehow the sun's warmth didn't penetrate the icy cold she felt inside.

Her worst nightmare. Troy had found out her assailant, who wasn't some stranger he could hate from a distance, but his own good friend, someone they'd both known. "What did you hear?" she asked in a dull voice.

"Well, for one thing, I heard that my leg is permanently screwed up. That I'll have to wear this boot for six months and I won't be able to drive or exercise. After that, I have to have some surgery that might or might not allow me to walk without a cane."

She didn't answer, couldn't. She could barely focus on what he was saying, only realizing that it had something to do with his leg not healing.

That awful name kept echoing through her head. *Jeremy. Jeremy. Jeremy.*

It whirled her back to a night she'd spent years trying to forget. To a very handsome and charming older guy who'd flattered her at her birthday celebration, walked her partway home, then dragged her into his apartment and spent what seemed like hours hurting her in ways she'd had no idea a man could hurt a woman.

Her screams had been ineffectual; the other apartments had been empty. Her pleas had fallen on deaf ears, even made him laugh.

What he'd done to her physically was horrible enough. But his name-calling, his degradation of her as a woman, his comments about her past, her unworthiness, her asking for it... All of those words had stuck to her like poison glue, growing inside her right along with the baby growing in her womb. The ugly descriptions of herself had expanded until they were all she could see, all she could feel.

Only the tireless nurturing of her aunt, and intensive sessions with a skilled therapist, had been able to pull her out of the deep depression she'd sunk into.

"You cheated on me," Troy said now. "And you lied to me."

Cheater. Liar. Even though the words Jeremy had uttered had been much stronger and more degrading, the echo in the voice of her beloved Troy made her double over, the hurt was so sudden and so strong.

She knelt in the dirt beside the truck, holding her stomach.

"Don't even try to defend yourself. I won't believe a word you say."

His flat, angry, judgmental certainty slammed into her. It was just the way she'd figured he would react; it was the reason she'd thrown clothes into a bag and left town the day she learned she was pregnant.

Now, though, her automatic reaction was different. To her own surprise, she didn't feel like running. She felt her shoulders go back as she glared at him. "Did you just tell me not to say anything?"

"Yeah," he said, leaning out of the truck, breathing hard. "That's exactly what I told you."

Gravel dug into her knees. What was she doing on her knees? Holding on to the side of the truck for support, she climbed to her feet. "Don't you ever tell me I can't say what's on my mind. I spent a lot of years keeping silent, and I'm tired of it. I don't deserve what happened to me, and I don't deserve for you to blame me for what someone else did to me."

He looked at her with huge sags under his eyes, as if he'd aged ten years. "You wanted to be with him. Right?"

Whoa! Just like Jeremy! Her hands went to her hips as heat flushed through her body. "You can stop right now with telling me what I did and didn't want. No woman would want what happened to me, and any man who says otherwise is messed up." She walked closer to him, her heart pounding in her ears. "You hear me? Totally. Messed. Up." With each word, she jabbed a pointing finger at him. "If that's what you're thinking, you can get out of my life."

He swung his legs down with a painful wince. "I'm

going, just as soon as I can get a ride. And you can get out of mine. I want your bags packed and you…" He trailed off, swallowed hard. "You and Xavier…off my property. By tomorrow."

Chapter Fourteen

Troy watched the woman he'd thought he loved draw in a rasping breath, then clench her jaw. "I'll drive you home," she said. "Let me get Xavier."

She turned before he could answer and marched down toward the playing field. Her back was straight, shoulders squared.

He stared after her, then squeezed his eyes shut and looked away. His heart rebelled against the sudden change he was asking of it: stop loving her, start hating her. Stop believing in her, realize that she'd been lying this whole time.

She *had* been lying, right? Because she'd said she hadn't known her assailant, but when he'd confronted her with Jeremy's name, she'd tacitly acknowledged him as Xavier's father.

But why would she have lied about it being Jeremy?

The answer had to be that she'd gone with him willingly. Just as Jeremy's brother had said.

Sliding out of the truck, he landed painfully on his bad leg, and the metal cane the doctor had lent him— the old man's cane with four little feet on the end— crashed to the ground.

A teenage girl on a skateboard swooped down, picked it up, then skidded in a circle to hand it back to him.

He wasn't even man enough to pick up his wretched cane for himself.

Angelica came back, pulling an obviously reluctant and angry Xavier by the hand. "Mom!" he was whining, almost crying. "I don't want to go."

"Get in the truck," she ordered.

"But—"

"Now." Her voice was harsh.

Tears spilled from Xavier's eyes, and his lower lip pouted out, but he climbed into the truck.

"Mr. Troy!" Xavier said as soon as they were all in. "Mama says we have to move away. But that's not true, is it?"

Troy looked over at Angelica and saw a muscle twitch in her cheek. Her jaw was set and obviously she wasn't about to answer.

Troy was already regretting his hasty order that they leave. He turned back to Xavier, looked at his hopeful face.

Looked into Jeremy's eyes. How had he not noticed that before? "I'm sorry, but yes. You do have to leave."

"Why?" Xavier's face screwed up. "I love it here. I hate moving."

Troy looked over at Angelica and saw a single tear trickle down her cheek.

Well, sure, she was upset. Her game was up.

"Mom, you promised we wouldn't have to move again!"

Angelica cleared her throat. "I'm sorry, honey. I made a promise I couldn't keep."

"Seems you make a habit of that," Troy muttered.

Angelica's body gave the slightest little jerk, as if she'd been hit.

The truth hurt. He tried to work up some more righteous anger about that, but he was finding it hard to do.

What she'd done was wrong, but it had happened a long time ago.

But she's been lying to you just in the past few weeks.

But she'd seemed to genuinely care about him. Hadn't she? "Look," he said, "maybe I've overreacted. I...I need to take a breath, think about this. I don't want to throw the two of you out on the street..."

"We've been there before." She spun the truck around a corner too fast, making the tires squeal. "We'll manage."

"I don't want you to just manage. I need to pray about this, get right with God, figure things out. I was blindsided, but we all make mistakes. I...maybe I can work through it and learn to forgive you."

"Don't strain yourself." She pulled the truck into the long driveway and squealed to a jerky stop in front of his house. "Here you go."

There were a couple of unfamiliar cars parked in front of the house, and he couldn't deal with strangers. Didn't want to talk to anyone but Angelica. "I...Look. Let's talk before you go."

"I think you've said all you need to say. I know what you think about me. I know how much respect you have for me. All I want now is to pack my things and be gone."

"Mom! You should listen to Mr. Troy! Maybe we won't have to leave."

"Are you getting out?" she asked him through clenched teeth.

"No. Angelica—"

She pulled out fast enough to make the wheels spit gravel, drove past the kennels and down to the bunkhouse. She skidded to a halt and slammed the truck into park. "C'mom, Xavier. Out." As soon as the sobbing boy had obeyed, she faced Troy. "By tonight, we'll be gone." She slammed the truck's door and walked into the bunkhouse, back stiff, one arm around Xavier.

Troy sat in the truck, his legs and arms too heavy to move. He stared out at the cornfields and wondered what he could do now.

His life had been snatched out from under him. Instead of being active, doing everything himself, he'd need help. With the kennels. With his practice. Even with driving, for pity's sake. Instead of getting married to the woman he loved, instead of becoming dad to the child he'd come to care deeply for, he'd be alone.

Alone, with a big empty space in his heart.

He knew he shouldn't be sitting here feeling sorry for himself, but he couldn't seem to make himself move. He didn't know what to do next.

Well, he did know: he should pray, put it in God's hands.

He let his face fall forward into his hands. *God...* He didn't know how to ask or what to say. Even looking at the bunkhouse and knowing that Xavier and Angelica were inside packing made his throat tighten up and his heart ache.

Help, he prayed.

The word echoed in his mind, as if God was saying it back to him.

There was nothing to do but try to help them. He'd help them load their stuff into the truck, as much as a crippled guy could. Find someone to drive them to the station. He'd pay for tickets wherever they wanted to go.

Where would they go, though?

And what about follow-ups to Xavier's treatments? What would Angelica do for a job? She'd worried that this would happen, that the "us" wouldn't work out and that she'd be alone, unable to afford the rest of the cost of treatment. He'd waved her concern aside.

Had she suspected he'd find out the truth about her?

What *was* the truth about her? He pounded the seat beside him. Why had she cheated on him? Why had she given herself to Jeremy?

"Mr. Troy! Mr. Troy! Come in here!"

At first he thought he was imagining the sound, but no; it was Xavier pounding on the truck's door. He lowered the window and looked out. "You okay, kiddo?"

"I am, but Lily's not! She's having her puppies! And Mom says she's in trouble!"

Troy grabbed the bag he always kept in the backseat and swung out of the vehicle.

"Come on! Mom said you wouldn't still be here, but I knew you would!"

They hurried into the bunkhouse together and there in a dark corner of the living room was Angelica, leaning over Lily.

Her dark hair was pulled back with a rubber band and she was doing something with a towel.

"What's going on?"

"She's having trouble with this last one." The anger was gone from her voice, replaced by worry. "She can't get it out. I've been trying to help her, but I'm afraid of hurting the puppy."

"Let me see." He squatted down and saw the puppy's hindquarters protruding from Lily, who was whimpering and bending, trying to lick at the new puppy while three other pups pushed at her teats.

"Get a couple towels," he told Xavier, and to Angelica, "Get the surgical scissors out of my bag while I try to ease the pup out."

It took several minutes, and when the puppy was finally born he saw why: it was half again as big as the other puppies. Lily sank back, too exhausted for the usual maternal duties, so Troy carefully removed the sac and cut the cord and rubbed the puppy vigorously in a clean towel until he was sure it was breathing on its own.

"Poor thing," Angelica cooed, stroking Lily's ears and head. "You did a good job."

The pup was breathing well, so Troy tucked it against Lily's tummy, where it rooted blindly until it found a teat to latch on to.

Lily lifted her head feebly and licked the new puppy a couple of times, then dropped her head back to the floor.

"You can rest now," Angelica said to the tired dog. "We'll help you."

A small hand tugged at his shoulder as Xavier peered past him to look at Lily. "Is she gonna die? Why's she bleeding?"

He'd half forgotten that Xavier was there. "She's doing great. There's always a little blood when a dog gives birth, but she should be just fine."

"The puppies look...yucky."

Troy glanced over at Angelica, not sure how much detail she wanted her son to know. She shrugged, so he gave Xavier a barebones account of placentas and amniotic fluid and umbilical cords.

Fortunately the boy took it in stride. "Is she gonna have more?"

"I feel one more little bump, so she'll probably have

one more." He smiled at Xavier. "It'll be okay. Just takes a while."

"Can I watch?"

Troy looked over at Angelica, eyebrows raised.

"Sure, I guess." She stood up, stretched with her hands on her lower back, then walked over to the small bookcase. And started putting books in boxes.

Troy's heart dove down to his boots. For a minute there, he'd forgotten their conflict, forgotten that he'd kicked her out, forgotten they weren't a couple anymore. He opened his mouth to say something and then shut it again.

Should he take back his request that she leave? Beg her to stay? If she stayed, what would they do? Because the fact remained, she'd betrayed him.

Lily whimpered, and he looked down at her and petted and soothed her.

And then it hit him. Again. His revelation about how Angelica had cringed and held back from the physical.

If she'd consented to the relationship with Jeremy, then why did she act like an abused animal when a man tried to touch her?

Her phone buzzed just then, and he watched her as she answered it, wondering what to believe. Saw her frown and look despairingly at the half-filled box of books. "Are you sure you can't manage it? I'm kind of busy here."

She listened again.

"Okay. No, of course I can help." She clicked off the phone and sighed. "Lou Ann needs me to help her with something up at the house. Says she needs a woman, that you won't do. Can you…"

"I'll stay with Lily. And Xavier can stay with me."

He felt so good being able to do something for her. Lord help him, he wanted to take care of her. Still.

"All right. I'll be as quick as possible. I still want to get going by nightfall."

"Angelica—"

"No time to talk." And she was out the door.

Angelica stalked into the house with her fists clenched and teeth gritted tight against the tears that wanted to pour out of her. "Lou Ann!" she called past the lump in her throat.

"Out here," came a voice from the backyard.

She walked through the kitchen, trying not to look at the table where she and Xavier had shared so many meals with Troy. The counter where they'd leaned together, talking. The window through which she'd watched him playing ball with her son.

The whole place was soaked in memories, and if she and Xavier weren't going to have Troy, if this wasn't going to work, then it was best for them to get out of here now.

She walked through the back door.

"Surprise!"

The sounds of female laughter, the pretty white tablecloth over a round table decorated with flowers, the banner congratulating her and Troy...all of it was totally overwhelming.

She looked around at Lou Ann; Daisy; Xavier's teacher, Susan Hayashi; Miss Minnie Falcon from the Senior Towers; and her two best friends from Boston, Imani and Ruth. She burst into tears.

Immediately the women surrounded her. "It's a surprise shower!"

"We're so happy for you!"

"Aw, she's so emotional!"

"Wait a minute." Lou Ann broke through the squealing circle of women to step right in front of Angelica and look at her face. "Honey, what's wrong?"

Something in her voice made the rest of the women quiet down. Angelica looked into Lou Ann's calm brown eyes and bit her lip. "It's not going to work. Xavier and I are leaving."

"What?" The older woman looked shocked, and around her, gasps and words of dismay echoed in Angelica's ears.

"Come on, sit down and tell us about it," her friend Imani said.

"I think I'll head over to see Troy." The deep voice belonged to Dion, and he waved a hand and headed for the front of the house.

"Go on, we'll catch up with you later," Lou Ann said. "He was helping us set up the canopy," she explained to Angelica.

"What did you mean, you're leaving?" Daisy asked.

So, haltingly, hesitatingly, Angelica explained what had driven her and Troy apart. What was the point in hiding it all now? And they'd be gone, so if any gossip came from this good group of women—which she doubted—it wouldn't hurt Xavier.

"But God's good," she finished, choking out the words. "It looks like Xavier's going to get well."

Hugs and tears and murmurs of support surrounded her.

"Men can be such idiots." Daisy pulled her chair closer to Angelica and squeezed her hand. "My brother most of all."

"That jerk Jeremy most of all," her friend Ruth said.

"So I don't *need* to marry Troy anymore, to help

Xavier," Angelica explained, her voice still scratchy. "I mean, of course, he still wants a dad. But he's got time now, and he's got his health. And I can't be with someone who doesn't trust me."

"But what do you *want*?" Imani took her hand. "If Xavier weren't in the equation, would you love Troy? Do you want to be married to him?"

Angelica shut her eyes, and a slide show of memories played through her head.

The first time he'd asked her out, when she'd thought he must be joking, that no one as handsome and rich and popular as Troy could possibly want someone like her.

Riding horses together. Going to her first superfancy restaurant. Looking up to see his marriage proposal in skywriting, in front of the whole town.

Back then, she'd been in love in a naive way. Impressed with him, infatuated with him. And down on herself, seeing no alternatives.

Now things were different. She'd gotten through the past six years by relying on God's strength. With His help, she'd mothered Xavier through the worst moments a child could have and come out stronger. She'd built friendships like those with Ruth and Imani, who'd come all the way from Boston to celebrate a milestone. Now she could add Daisy and Lou Ann to that circle of lifetime friends.

Now she didn't *need* Troy. But the thought of life without him was colorless, plain, lonely.

Now her images of him were different. She thought of him not only helping her get rid of a drunken Buck but also giving her cola and comfort and a shoulder to cry on afterward. She thought of him bent over Bull in the road, caring for the wounded animal and still remembering her son's feelings. Thought of him admitting he'd been wrong to accuse her of still dating Buck, apologizing, going on to find Dr. Ravi for Xavier.

"If he could accept my past without thinking less of me, then yeah." She looked around at the circle of concerned, supportive faces. "Yeah. I still love him."

"All right," Lou Ann said. "Then we've got to find a way to make this right."

A sharp rap on the door made Troy's heart thump in double time: *Angelica*. Maybe she'd decided not to go. Maybe she wanted to talk to him.

He didn't know why he was so eager for that when she'd betrayed him with Jeremy. *If* she'd betrayed him. Because now that his initial anger was fading, he was having a hard time believing that of her.

"I know you're in there, my man," came Dion's deep voice.

"Come on in." Although he was glad to see his friend, needed a friend, Troy couldn't hide his disappointment.

Dion walked in looking anything but friendly. "Angelica's a mess. What did you do to her?"

Troy gave a tiny headshake, nodding toward Xavier. "We're watching Lily. She just had her last pup, and we're making sure she's okay."

"I'm helping," Xavier chimed in, bumping his shoulder against Troy. "Right, Mr. Troy?"

"Yep." Troy could barely choke out the word. How was he going to let this kid go?

Dion narrowed his eyes at Troy and flipped on the television to an old Western, complete with flaming arrows, bareback-riding Navajos and gun-toting cowboys. "Take a look, Xavier. You ever seen a cowboy show before?"

"Angelica wouldn't let…" Troy broke off. A little old-fashioned violence wouldn't hurt the kid. Xavier was immediately engrossed, leaving Dion and Troy free to move to an out-of-earshot spot at the kitchen table.

"What happened?" Dion glared at him.

Troy sighed, laced his hands together. "I found out who Xavier's dad is."

Dion looked at him expectantly.

"Jeremy Filmore."

Dion reared back and stared. "No kidding?"

Troy nodded. "No wonder she didn't want me to know, right? She could hardly claim assault with Jeremy." As he spoke, his anger came bubbling back.

"What do you mean? Does she say he attacked her?"

Troy nodded impatiently. "That's what she says, but I knew Jeremy. He wouldn't have done that."

Dion drummed his fingers on the table, frowning. "You sure about that, man?"

"You're not?"

"He had a pretty bad drinking problem." Dion studied the ceiling. "And he wasn't above clashing with the law. I broke up a few bar fights he started."

"True." And Troy had heard a few rumors, come to think of it, about how awful Jeremy had been to his wife.

"Not only that," Dion said, "but I was on duty for the car crash he died in. He was dead drunk. We didn't publicize that, and it was never in the paper—what would have been the point, when he was the only one involved, except to make his kids feel bad? But I can tell you it's so. I have the police reports to prove it."

"Wow." Jeremy, who'd had such potential, been a powerhouse of a football player, had died drunk. "So, what are you saying?"

"I'm saying that if Jeremy was drinking, he turned into an idiot. One who didn't have the ability to control himself."

"Even to the point of forcing himself on a woman?" The thought of Jeremy doing that to Angelica tapped in to a primal kind of outrage, but Troy fought to stay calm, to think. "Would he go that far, just because he wanted her?"

Dion shook his head. "It's about rage, not desire. They drill that into us at the police academy."

"But why would he be mad at Angelica? It just doesn't compute." Slowly he shook his head. "But it doesn't compute that she's lying, either."

"He was mad at women, period. Remember the so-called jokes he used to tell?"

"Yeah." Troy turned his cane over and over in his hand. "I guess I didn't spend much time with him once we were done with school."

"There could be another reason he kept his distance." The sound of televised gunshots and war whoops punctuated Dion's words. "He could have felt guilty about what he'd done."

"Getting her pregnant?"

"By force."

Troy pounded his fist on his knee.

"You have some apologizing to do."

Troy heaved out a sigh. "I screwed everything up."

"You might have, but pray Father God forgive you, and He will. Might even help you to make things right."

Troy nodded, staring down at the floor.

"And pray fast," Dion said. "Because there's a lot of estrogen coming our way."

Troy looked out the window Dion was looking out of. Marching in a line toward them, arms linked, were seven or eight women, his sister, Daisy, included. An-gelica was at the center, and she looked shell-shocked. The rest of the ladies just looked angry and determined.

Man, was he in for it! But at least Angelica was still here.

Just before the women got within earshot, Angelica pulled away. The other women gathered around her and seemed to be urging her forward, but she shook her head vehemently. Then she broke away from the women and climbed into his truck.

Daisy marched over and yanked open the truck door. She and Angelica exchanged words, and then Angelica slid over to the passenger seat.

Daisy climbed into the driver's seat and they drove away, leaving clouds of dust behind them.

It was a mark of how upset Troy was that he didn't even care that his reckless sister was driving his vehicle.

He just wanted to be in there with Angelica.

The women watched her go and then headed toward the bunkhouse, looking more serious and less angry now.

"You better go out there and face them," Dion advised.

Xavier pushed in between them to look out the window. "Those ladies look mad."

"I know. But they're not mad at you, buddy." He spoke the reassuring words automatically, but his mind wasn't on Xavier. Mostly he wanted to know where Angelica had gone.

As the women reached the bunkhouse, he went out the front door and stood on the porch, arms crossed.

"You stay in here with me, Little Bit," he heard Dion say behind him.

The women stood in a line in front of Troy. "Come

down here," said a dark-skinned woman he'd never seen before.

Troy used his cane to make his way halfway down the front steps.

"You've hurt that girl something terrible," Lou Ann said.

The dark-skinned woman added, "You accused her of stuff she didn't do."

"She'd never have cheated on you."

"I...yeah." Troy sat down on the edge of the porch and let his head sink into his hands. He was only now realizing the enormity of what he'd done. He'd made a terrible mistake, maybe lost the best part of his life— Xavier and Angelica. He looked up. "Where'd Angelica go?"

The women consulted and murmured among themselves for a couple of minutes. "We think she went out Highway 93," Lou Ann said finally.

Dion came out behind him, clapped a hand on his shoulder. "If you want to follow her, I can drive you. But not if you're going to make a fool of yourself again."

"No promises. I've already been an idiot. But I want to tell her how sorry I am."

That seemed to make the women happy; there were a couple of approving nods. "Take him out there, Dion," Lou Ann said, "but keep an eye on him."

Angelica knelt at the white roadside cross. *Jeremy Filmore* was painted on the horizontal board; *In loving memory* on the vertical one.

It wasn't his grave, but this was where he'd had his fatal accident. Somehow it had seemed to make more sense to come here, to this place she'd driven by dozens of times, getting mad and hating him with each pass. Never before had she stopped, gotten out of the car and studied it.

Now she saw the plastic flowers, the kids' football, the baby shoe and picture that decorated the cross, all looking surprisingly new, given that he'd died almost five years ago.

It reminded her that Jeremy had had a life, kids, people who loved him enough to keep up a memorial.

How could he be loved when he'd done something so awful?

Her legs went weak and she sank to her knees as regret overcame her. If only she hadn't been drunk that night. If only he hadn't. If only a friend had walked home with them. If only Troy had come out with her.

She'd never understand the why of it, no way. Why had God let it happen, something so awful?

She sat back and hugged her knees to her chest, aching as she remembered the years of hating herself, all the loose, ugly clothes she'd taken to wearing, scared of provoking unwanted male attention. Afraid of being the tramp Jeremy had accused her of being.

"I wasted the best years of my life hating you!" she cried out, pounding the ground, as if Jeremy lay beneath the memorial, as if he could still feel pain. She wanted to hurt him as he'd hurt her. Wanted to make him feel ashamed and awful. Wanted him to lose the love of his life, the way she'd lost Troy, twice now.

"Hey," Daisy said, getting out of the truck. "You okay?"

Angelica kept her eyes closed, her whole body tense as a coiled spring. "I hate him," she said. "I can't make myself stop hating him. I can't forgive him. I thought I could, but I can't."

Daisy knelt and put an arm around her. "He was

awful. A complete jerk. No one deserves to be treated the way you were treated."

"I hate him, hate him, hate him! I want him to suffer like I did. I want him to lose everything."

"Can't blame you there. Stinks that he lived in the community like a good person, and meanwhile, you felt like you had to leave."

"Yeah."

A breeze kicked up, and a few leaves fell around them. Fall was coming. Maybe it was already here.

Something was tugging at her. She thought about the years since the assault. "I hurt a lot in the past seven years."

"I know you must have."

"But I also had Xavier and got closer to God and… and grew up. Where Jeremy…he must have always had this in the back of his mind, what he did."

"Nah." Daisy let out a snort. "Guys like that are jerks. He didn't suffer."

"I think he did suffer. I think that's one reason he drank so much."

"Don't try to humanize him. It's okay to hate the guy who assaulted you!"

Angelica hugged Daisy; half laughing through her tears. "You're wonderful. But I don't actually think that it *is* okay to hate."

Daisy rolled her eyes. "Don't go all holy on me."

"I'm not very holy at all." Angelica shifted from her knees to a more comfortable sitting position. "I've always felt guilty myself, because I…" Tears rose to her eyes again. "Because I dressed up pretty and flirted with all the guys at the bar. Including Jeremy." She could barely squeeze the words out past the lump in her throat.

"Oh, give me a break. Men flirt every day and no woman commits assault on them. It wasn't fair, what happened to you." Daisy squeezed her shoulder. "And you totally didn't deserve it."

"You don't think so?"

"No! You'd probably make different decisions today, and you'd probably see more red flags with Jeremy." Daisy's voice went into social-worker mode. "Our brains keep developing and learn from experience. But no way—no *way*—did you deserve to be raped. Whether you flirt or dress up or get drunk, no means no." She squeezed Angelica's shoulder. "And you have to forgive yourself for being a silly twenty-one-year-old."

Daisy's words washed over her like a balm.

If she could forgive herself—the way God forgave her—then maybe she could forgive Jeremy. And get on with her life.

But it wasn't easy. "I'm still mad at myself. And even though I'm figuring it out, I still feel pretty hostile toward Jeremy."

Daisy was weaving a handful of clovers into a long chain. "I have a terrible temper," she said. "Pastor Ricky always tells me that forgiveness is a decision, not a feeling."

Forgiveness is a decision, not a feeling. The words echoed in her mind with the ring of truth.

Behind them, a truck lumbered by, adding a whiff of diesel to the air.

Forgiveness is a decision, not a feeling.

Angelica reached out a finger to the baby shoe that hung on the crossbar. "I know, I've known all along, that God worked it for good by giving me Xavier." She drew in a breath. "Okay. I forgive you, Jeremy."

"And yourself?" Daisy prompted.

"I forgive…I forgive myself, too."

No fireworks exploded, and no church bells rang. But a tiny flower of peace took seed in Angelica's heart. For now, it was enough.

"Now, don't go ballistic," Dion warned Troy. "I think I see Angelica and Daisy up there."

"Why are they out of the car on the highway?"

"They're by a roadside memorial." Dion paused, then added, "For Jeremy Filmore."

Troy's hands balled into fists as Dion slowed the truck to a crawl and drove slowly past Daisy and Angelica. "If this doesn't show she's got feelings for him—"

"I'm sure she does have feelings." Dion pulled the truck off the road and turned off the ignition. "Wouldn't you hate the guy that did what he did?"

"That's not what I—" And Troy stopped. He was doing it again, being a jerk. He had to stop jumping to conclusions about Angelica, about how she felt and what she was doing. It wasn't fair to her or to him or to Xavier.

He sat there and watched while Daisy and Angelica held hands and prayed together. Man, his sister was a good person.

And so was Angelica. Talking with Dion had confirmed what his heart had already suspected: No way would she cheat on him.

He was a fool.

Troy dropped his head into his hands. If Angelica was praying, he should do that, too. She was amazing, always plunging forward and trying to do the right thing, to make a change, to live the way she was supposed to despite the horrible circumstances life always seemed to be throwing at her.

And he, what did he do?

He got his feelings hurt and suffered a minor disability and he fell apart.

He'd tried to fix her life and Xavier's on his own, giving her a job, letting them live on his place, getting medical help, even the marriage proposal. Looking back, it seemed as if he'd been waving his arms around uselessly, acting like some comic-book hero, trying to fix problems way too big for him.

For the first time in his life, he saw—just dimly— that there might be another way. The way that gave Dion his uncanny peacefulness. The way that made Angelica able to kneel by that jerk Jeremy's memorial and pray, after all she'd suffered.

He wanted, needed, that ability to let God in, to trust Him. Most of all, to ask Him for help. To recognize that he himself wasn't God and that God could do better than he could on his own poor human strength.

I'm sorry, God. Help me do better.

It was a simple prayer, but when he lifted his head, he felt some kind of peace. And when he looked over at Dion, he saw his friend smile. "What do you say I take Daisy home so you and Angelica can have some time?" he asked.

"That's a good idea."

Troy got out of the truck then and limped over to the two women. When he got there, Daisy stood and studied his face. Then, nodding as if satisfied, she walked back toward Dion's truck.

Leaving Troy to kneel beside Angelica.

She finished her prayer, turned and looked at him.

Eyes full of wisdom but guarded against the pain he might inflict.

He reached out hesitantly and touched her dark hair. She didn't flinch away. Just studied his face.

A car whizzed by behind them. Another. The sound faded away into the horizon, and quiet fell.

He looked down at the cross for Jeremy. A man who'd done something so horrendous to the woman he loved. Reflexively his fist clenched. "I could kill him."

Angelica reached out and put her hand over his. "He's gone. Leave it to God." Her voice shook a little, and when he looked away from Jeremy's cross and into her eyes, he saw that they were shiny with tears.

One overflowed, rolled down her cheek. "You kicked us out. You didn't believe me."

"I'm so sorry." He relaxed his fist and reached out slowly to thumb the tears away. "I love you. I never stopped loving you. Can you forgive me?"

There was a moment's silence. Long enough for him to feel the cooling breeze against his back and smell the sweet, pungent zing of ozone. It was going to rain.

"I don't know." She knelt there, her face still wet with tears, and studied him seriously. As though she was trying to read him. "I love you, too, Troy. But I can't live with being distrusted, and I can't live with someone who thinks I'm a bad person inside."

"You're the best person I know!" The words burst out of him and he realized they were the exact truth. She'd gone through so much, and with such faith, and there was humility and wisdom and dignity in every move she made, every word she spoke. "Look, I screwed up, and I screwed up bad. I want to spend the rest of my life making it up to you. Even that won't be enough, but I want to try."

"Really?"

"Yeah, really." He touched her hand, tentatively, carefully. "I can't guarantee I'll never make another mistake, but I can guarantee it won't be about who you are inside."

She didn't look convinced.

He blundered on. "Like, I tend to be jealous."

She lifted an eyebrow. "No kidding. Right?"

"It's just, I know how incredible you are, and I see other men seeing it, and it makes me crazy."

Her lips tightened. "I'm not flattered by that, Troy. It's not a good thing."

"I know. I'm willing to do whatever I need to do to fix this. Read self-help books. Get counseling. Join Dion's men's group at church."

"That," she said instantly. "That's what you need. Other men to rein you in when you go all macho."

"I'll call him tomorrow." He took both of her hands in his. "Look, Angelica, I'm nowhere near as good of a person as you are. But I need you to know that I'll do everything in my power to protect you and Xavier. I'll take care of you and love you for the rest of my days. And I will never, ever tell you to leave again."

She looked steadily into his eyes as if she was reading him, judging him. And she had the right. She had to protect her son.

Finally her face broke into a smile. "I'm not a better person than you are. I've made plenty of mistakes and I'm sure I'll make more."

"Does this mean…" He trailed off, hardly daring to hope.

To his shock, she laughed, a pure, joyous sound. "You caught me on the right day," she said. "I'm on a forgiveness roll."

He took her face in his hands and was blown away by the sheer goodness of who she was. "I don't deserve you. You're…you're amazing, inside and out. I…" He ran out of words. *Way to go, Hinton. Smooth with the ladies, as always.*

She lifted her eyebrows, a tiny smile quirking the corner of her mouth. "Does this mean… What does this mean?"

She looked at peace about whether he wanted to marry her or not, whether they had a future or not. She had that glow of faith. She'd always had it, but it glowed brighter now.

He had so much to learn from her. And what could he, with his gimpy leg and his ignorant rages and his general guy immaturity, offer her?

Little enough, but if he could ease her parenting burdens and listen to her problems and protect her from anyone—anyone!—who so much as looked sideways at her, he wanted to do it. Would devote his life to doing it.

"It means," he said, "that I want you to marry me. For real. Forever. I want to help you and support you and be Xavier's dad. And I want it for the rest of our lives, through thickheadedness and illness and whatever else life throws at us. If you'll have me."

She looked at him with love glowing in her eyes. "Of course I will."

And as they embraced, the sky opened up and a warm, gentle rain started to fall, offering God's blessing on their new beginning.

Chapter Fifteen

"That was awesome, Mom!"

Angelica turned toward her son's excited voice, only slightly slowed down by her wedding dress. Pure white. Traditional. What she'd always wanted.

"What was awesome, honey? The wedding?"

"No, the ride in a Hummer!"

Of course, her healthy, normal son had loved their unorthodox ride back from the church more than fidgeting through the wedding ceremony and receiving line.

Now they were back at the farm for the reception, which Lou Ann had insisted on orchestrating. There were two canopies set up, in case the warm October sunshine turned to rain, and Angelica could smell the good hearty dinner that was on buffet tables for the guests.

A small wedding, but meaningful. Just what she'd hoped for…and for many years hadn't dreamed possible for herself.

Since forgiving Jeremy that day by the side of the road, since feeling the sincerity of Troy's love and belief in her, she'd felt light enough to fly.

Gramps hustled over to give her a hug. "Did I tell you how beautiful you look?"

"About a dozen times, but it's okay." She kissed his grizzled cheek. "Thank you for walking me down the aisle. You've been wonderful today. I'm so grateful."

"Not sure about the rest of those Hintons, but Troy is all right." Troy had tried to talk Gramps into moving out of the Senior Towers and into the bunkhouse. When Gramps had refused, insisting on staying with his friends, Troy had helped him move into a bigger apartment at the Towers, paying the difference in rent secretly to save the old man's pride.

That was part of what she loved about Troy: he was willing to change, to break from the long-held Hinton animosity toward Gramps, to embrace her family with all its flaws.

Lou Ann had ridden from the church with Troy's father. As she emerged, radiant in a maroon dress and hat, from Mr. Hinton's vintage Cadillac, Gramps sniffed. "I'm gonna go over there and make sure he's not bothering Lou Ann. He always did have a crush on her."

People were all arriving now, and Angelica watched Lou Ann rush away from both men with an eye roll, hurrying on to direct the caterers and welcome guests. Angelica hadn't wanted a big fancy reception, but thanks to Lou Ann, everything was simple and perfect, from the centerpieces—a pretty mix of sunflowers, orange dahlias and autumn leaves—to the bluegrass band strumming lively music.

"Hey, Mom, look!" Xavier came out of the kennels, his suit knees dusty. "I have a 'prise for you!"

"You'll want to watch this," Troy said, coming up behind her. He wrapped his arms around her middle and she swayed back against him. He made her dizzy…in a good way. A very good way.

"Mom, pay attention!" Xavier stood frowning, hands on hips.

Troy chuckled into her ear, and Angelica laughed with self-conscious delight. It amazed her that she could feel so attracted to Troy, that it was easy and good to be close to him. No more cringing, no more fear. She trusted him completely.

She was getting back the girl she'd been, with God's help. He truly did make all things new.

She eased herself over to Troy's side, where she could breathe a little more easily. "What's the surprise, sweetie?" she called to her son.

"Lily's dressed up for the wedding!" Xavier yelled, so loud that everyone turned to see.

The rescued pit bull, her collar decorated with yellow roses, emerged from the barn with a line of puppies behind her. Amid the happy murmur of the guests, Xavier's voice rang out again. "Look what else!"

He whistled, and Bull came running full tilt from the barn.

Angelica did a double take. How was Bull moving so fast?

And then she realized that his back legs were supported by a doggie wheelchair, also decorated with yellow and white flowers. As he zigzagged after Xavier, Angelica pressed her hands to her mouth, amazed.

"We've been practicing with him for a couple of weeks," Troy said. "Xavier was determined that Bull could come to the wedding and play."

And trust Troy to make it happen, to take the time to work with Xavier and the dog and to keep the surprise for her.

"Come and get it, everyone!" Lou Ann called, and people flowed toward the tables to eat, stopping to greet them on the way. And there were hugs. So many hugs.

As she and Troy stood there arm in arm, welcoming their guests, Angelica lifted her face to the afternoon sunshine and thanked God for all He'd done for them.

Xavier barreled up toward them, and at the same time, both Troy and Angelica reached out to hold him. "Our whole family," Angelica said, rubbing her son's head, roughened by newly sprouted hair. Joy bubbled up inside her, rich and full and satisfying.

"Well…" Troy said, sounding guilty.

"Mom? There's one other thing. Dad and I have been talking about it."

"What?" She stepped out of Troy's embrace to frown in mock exasperation at her two men. "Are you guys conspiring against me?"

"What's 'spiring?"

"Hatching a secret plan, buddy. And…kinda. Tell her, Zavey."

Her son reached out and took one of her hands and one of Troy's. "I want a little sister."

"Oh, Zavey Davey…" She looked up at Troy as her mind flashed back to a family she'd seen in the park. Mom, Dad and two children, one an adorable little girl. She hadn't thought it was possible God could be so good to her, but now she knew He could.

The last of her old doubts about the future faded away at the sight of Troy's smile. "What do you think?"

"I think it's a distinct possibility." He gave her a quick wink and reached out to pull her back into his arms.

* * * * *

Dear Reader,

Cancer, violent crime, broken relationships… Most of us have been touched by at least one of these difficult challenges. Life in this world isn't always easy or pretty. Angelica suffered terribly at the hands of her assailant and struggled to care for her son during his illness. But she maintained her faith throughout her struggles, and her hard times were redeemed in her love for Xavier and ultimately in her new family with Troy.

I've faced challenges in my own life and have struggled to understand why God allows us to suffer. We may never fully understand God's ways. But I've learned that walking with God through life's challenges brings me closer to Him than easy, happy times ever could.

How fortunate we are to be able to rely on a loving God who helps us cope with and grow through our hard times, and who works all things for good.

Wishing you peace,
Lee

COMING NEXT MONTH FROM
Love Inspired®

Available March 17, 2015

AMISH REDEMPTION
Brides of Amish Country • by Patricia Davids

Joshua Bowman saves Mary Kauffman from a tornado—and is immediately taken with the Amish single mom. But will falling for the sheriff's daughter mean revealing the secrets that haunt his past?

REUNITED WITH THE COWBOY
Refuge Ranch • by Carolyne Aarsen

Heather Bannister returns home to Montana and comes face-to-face with old love John Argall. When the single dad needs her to babysit his young daughter, can she stop their old feelings from rekindling?

A DAD FOR HER TWINS
Family Ties • by Lois Richer

Abby McDonald lost her husband, her job and her house. Accepting cowboy Cade Lebret's offer to stay at his ranch could mean a daddy for her twins and a new love for the young mom-to-be.

FINALLY A HERO
The Rancher's Daughters • by Pamela Tracy

His troubled life behind him, Jesse Campbell's concentrating on giving his son a better life than he had. But could opening his heart for ranch manager Eva Hubrecht mean having the family he's always dreamed of?

SMALL-TOWN BACHELOR
by Jill Kemerer

After a storm devastates her town, Claire Sheffield organizes the reconstruction with help from project manager Reed Hamilton. She's drawn to his skill and generosity, but can she convince this city boy to give up the bright lights for her?

COAST GUARD COURTSHIP
by Lisa Carter

Braeden Scott is done with relationships. But when his landlord's daughter, Amelia Duer, sails into his life, will this Coast Guard lieutenant discover his safe harbor with the girl next door?

LOOK FOR THESE AND OTHER LOVE INSPIRED BOOKS WHEREVER BOOKS ARE SOLD, INCLUDING MOST BOOKSTORES, SUPERMARKETS, DISCOUNT STORES AND DRUGSTORES.

LICNM0315

REQUEST YOUR FREE BOOKS!

2 FREE INSPIRATIONAL NOVELS
PLUS 2
FREE
MYSTERY GIFTS

Love Inspired®

YES! Please send me 2 FREE Love Inspired® novels and my 2 FREE mystery gifts (gifts are worth about $10). After receiving them, if I don't wish to receive any more books, I can return the shipping statement marked "cancel." If I don't cancel, I will receive 6 brand-new novels every month and be billed just $4.74 per book in the U.S. or $5.24 per book in Canada. That's a saving of at least 21% off the cover price. It's quite a bargain! Shipping and handling is just 50¢ per book in the U.S. and 75¢ per book in Canada.* I understand that accepting the 2 free books and gifts places me under no obligation to buy anything. I can always return a shipment and cancel at any time. Even if I never buy another book, the two free books and gifts are mine to keep forever.

105/305 IDN F47Y

Name _____ (PLEASE PRINT) _____

Address _____ Apt. #

City _____ State/Prov. _____ Zip/Postal Code

Signature (if under 18, a parent or guardian must sign)

Mail to the **Harlequin® Reader Service:**
IN U.S.A.: P.O. Box 1867, Buffalo, NY 14240-1867
IN CANADA: P.O. Box 609, Fort Erie, Ontario L2A 5X3

**Are you a subscriber to Love Inspired books
and want to receive the larger-print edition?
Call 1-800-873-8635 or visit www.ReaderService.com.**

* Terms and prices subject to change without notice. Prices do not include applicable taxes. Sales tax applicable in N.Y. Canadian residents will be charged applicable taxes. Offer not valid in Quebec. This offer is limited to one order per household. Not valid for current subscribers to Love Inspired books. All orders subject to credit approval. Credit or debit balances in a customer's account(s) may be offset by any other outstanding balance owed by or to the customer. Please allow 4 to 6 weeks for delivery. Offer available while quantities last.

Your Privacy—The Harlequin® Reader Service is committed to protecting your privacy. Our Privacy Policy is available online at www.ReaderService.com or upon request from the Harlequin Reader Service.

We make a portion of our mailing list available to reputable third parties that offer products we believe may interest you. If you prefer that we not exchange your name with third parties, or if you wish to clarify or modify your communication preferences, please visit us at www.ReaderService.com/consumerschoice or write to us at Harlequin Reader Service Preference Service, P.O. Box 9062, Buffalo, NY 14269. Include your complete name and address.

LI13R

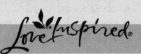
Hannah edged closer to her. "I don't like storms."

Mary slipped an arm around her daughter. "Don't
worry. We'll be at Katie's house before the rain catches
us."

It turned out she was wrong. Big raindrops began hitting her windshield. A strong gust of wind shook the
buggy and blew dust across the road. The sky grew
darker by the minute. She urged Tilly to a faster pace. She
should have stayed home.

A red car flew past her with the driver laying on the
horn. Tilly shied and nearly dragged the buggy into the
fence along the side of the road. Mary managed to right
her. "Foolish *Englischers*. We are over as far as we can
get."

The rumble of thunder became a steady roar behind
them. Tilly broke into a run. Hannah began screaming.
Mary glanced back and her heart stopped. A tornado had
dropped from the clouds and was bearing down on them.
Dust and debris flew out from the wide base.

Dear God, help me save my baby. What do I do?

She saw an intersection up ahead.

Bracing her legs against the dash, she pulled back on the lines, trying to slow Tilly enough to make the corner without overturning. The mare seemed to sense the plan. She slowed and made the turn with the buggy tilting on two wheels. Mary grabbed Hannah and held on to her. Swerving wildly behind the horse, the buggy finally came back onto all four wheels. Before the mare could gather speed again, a man jumped into the road waving his arms. He grabbed Tilly's bridle and pulled her to a stop.

Shouting, he pointed toward an abandoned farmhouse. "There's a cellar on the south side."

Mary jumped out of the buggy and pulled Hannah into her arms. The man was already unhitching Tilly, so Mary ran toward the ramshackle structure. The wind threatened to pull her off her feet. The trees and even the grass were straining toward the approaching tornado. She reached the old cellar door, but couldn't lift it against the force of the wind. She was about to lie on the ground on top of Hannah when the man appeared at her side. Together, they were able to lift the door.

A second later, she was pushed down the steps into darkness.

Don't miss
AMISH REDEMPTION by Patricia Davids,
available April 2015 wherever
Love Inspired® books and ebooks are sold.

www.Harlequin.com